THE

CHRISTMAS

DONUT

REVOLUTION

A Novel by

Gregg Sapp

THE CHRISTMAS DONUT REVOLUTION
Holidazed – Book 2
Copyright © 2019 by Gregg Sapp

FIRST EDITION SOFTCOVER
ISBN: 162253509X
ISBN-13: 978-1-62253-509-5

Editor: Lane Diamond
Cover Artist: Kabir Shah
Interior Designer: Lane Diamond

EVOLVED PUBLISHING™
www.EvolvedPub.com
Butler, Wisconsin, USA

Printed in Book Antiqua font.

BOOKS BY GREGG SAPP

HOLIDAZED
Book 1: *Halloween from the Other Side*
Book 2: *The Christmas Donut Revolution*
Book 3: *Upside Down Independence Day*

Fresh News Straight from Heaven

Dollarapalooza
(or "The Day Peace Broke Out in Columbus")

DEDICATION

To Kelsey and Keegan,
for so many Christmas memories...
and donuts!

CHAPTER 1
Columbus, Ohio – December 19, 2012

4:30 AM

Every morning, Huck Carp motivated himself to get out of bed by thinking the same thought—maybe today will be *the day*. He truly expected it "any day now," just as Edgar had promised a year ago at an Occupy Columbus rally. So far, its arrival had defied all predictions and expectations. Still, Huck remained convinced that one fair day, very soon, something monumental would happen—some trigger, catalyst, or a straw of such gross injustice that it would break the back of the oppressive kleptocratic social order—and then, finally, the *revolution* would begin.

If not for that, why get out of bed at all?

Huck shivered under layers of blankets, trying to summon the courage to rise. He knew that with his first upright step into the concrete of his basement apartment, frigid air would slam him like a sudden plunge into ice water. In December, no matter how high he set the thermostat, the gurgling old boiler couldn't keep up, and the overnight temperature in his room dipped so low that his breath steamed. The trick was to move fast.

He skittered into the bathroom, and turned on the space heater and the hot water even before flipping the light switch. When he looked at himself in the mirror, he noticed tiny frost crystals in his thin eyebrows. His cheeks were numb, and his skin looked pasty, the tone and texture of a peeled banana. This, he told himself, constituted suffering for The Cause. He wondered when it would be enough.

Showering was something of a guilty pleasure, being indulgent and wasteful of natural resources.

Okay... sure... somewhat.

This was less true in the winter, since he legitimately needed the hot spray to restore sensation to his skin and fervor to his soul. Still, when he recalled those chilly mornings camped out the Ohio Statehouse lawn with his Occupy Columbus cohort, everybody freezing and filthy, but flaunting their discomfort and sediment like badges of honor, he couldn't completely shake the feeling that his daily shower was a sellout.

Maybe that's part of the reason the Occupy movement failed.

He had to admit that its foot soldiers stank rather badly, which tended to undermine their message.

Huck dried himself in the shower stall and reached out to grab his clothes hanging on the backside of the bathroom door, then got dressed in there, too. In the process of buttoning his shirt, he snapped the last frayed thread holding on a middle button. He held it between thumb and forefinger and stared, stymied as to what to do next. He owned neither a needle nor thread, and even if he did, sewing it back on would've been, to him, an undertaking on the order of solving a Rubik's Cube. Instead, he stapled the folds of his shirt together and hoped nobody would notice. Maybe later, he could beg or cajole Ximena into fixing it for him.

He left the bathroom, carried the space heater into the kitchen, careful not to trip over its long extension cord, and placed it on top of the mini-fridge, next to the two-cup coffee maker, which, per its programming, sputtered as it finished brewing. He took a gulp—the first cup of any day was gulped, not sipped—and rummaged through the fridge for a tub of yogurt and the remaining half of a bran muffin. After putting the coffee and yogurt on an overturned milk crate that served as his kitchen table, Huck sat on a three-legged stool, logged onto his tablet, and steadied it on his knee.

This half an hour before he had to catch his bus was the most intellectually productive period of his day. In one window on the tablet, he opened his personal journal in a Word document entitled "Reflections." In another window, he opened the homepage for the latest issue of *Social Text* and began reading while basking in the diabolized glow of the space heater. Whenever he found some assertion or conclusion in *Social Text* that raised a point he wanted to remember, he toggled back to his journal and made a note of it. Ironically, he did more research and studied harder now that he was a dropout than when he'd been a student. The difference was that now he did it for The Cause, so it served a higher purpose.

He stuffed an apple and some trail mix into his backpack, where he also kept his tablet, a Swiss Army knife, two joints in a coin purse, an all-purpose bandana, a first aid kit, a prescription bottle of sertraline, a copy of his self-published chapbook of poetry entitled *Verse for the Ninety-Nine Per Cent*, and the dog-eared paperback copy of *Ten Days that Changed the World* that Edgar had given him for his 21st birthday. He mentally checked off each item to ensure that he had them in case of need during the day, and then left the apartment.

The last thing that he did on his way out the door was turn the page on his Daily Worker desk calendar, pausing to note that on that same day, December the 19th in the year 1843, Charles Dickens published "A Christmas Carol." Huck had never thought of that story as belonging to the literary canon of socialism, but it kind of made sense, now that he thought about it. Marx was a fan of Dickens. They were pals, maybe even co-conspirators. Was there ever a more representative prole than Bob Cratchit? He was hard-working, long-suffering, and, although meek by nature, a perfect candidate for unionizing. Likewise, Scrooge's ghostly dreams clearly represented a Hegelian dialectic playing out in his unconscious.

The quotation cited on the calendar's page was a description of Scrooge: "Oh! but he was a tight-fisted hand at the grindstone, Scrooge! A squeezing, wrenching, grasping, scraping, clutching, covetous old sinner!"

Just like a typical capitalist! Bah, humbug, indeed.

5:00 AM

The first thing Chavonne Hayes did when she got out of bed was check Leon's wallet. Yesterday evening, he asked to borrow $20 from her for "a couple of beers with Bo." Now, she needed to know how much, if any, was left.

"What for do yo' need $20?" she had demanded when he asked for the money. "I just gave yo' $20 on Monday. Don't be tellin' me that yo' done spent all of it."

"I got just $8 bucks left."

"That ought to be enough for just a *couple* of beers."

"Baby, I'm only askin' jus' in case, like, say, s'pose the car breaks down an' I need to get me a cab."

"Ho, ain't that a story! What that means is that yo' *plan* to drink *more'n* a couple beers, an' then *gotta* take a cab on the cause that if yo' drive buzzed, not to mention with no insurance, the sheriff 'll haul yo' ass into jail. Tell me if that ain't what yo' be really thinkin'."

"Baby, like usual, you're right."

"Damn right I'm right!"

Although it had felt good to hear Leon say it, Chavonne wasn't entirely sure what it was he agreed that she was right about—that he understood the risks of driving impaired and uninsured, or that he fully intended to exceed his promise to drink only a "couple of beers." Leon was shrewd about getting his way, even while seeming to submit to hers.

Anyway, after making him say, "Please, please, please, Baby," she'd given up the $20, with the condition that he'd "damn sure best make it last 'til Friday." So, come morning, when she checked his wallet and found that it contained zero currency, her anger boiled over not because he'd spent every last dollar, but because he'd taken her warning so lightly.

Chavonne tossed the empty wallet at him in bed. "Don't yo' ask for no more money tonight, hear me, Leon?"

Leon was either sound asleep or pretending to be. Either way, it would have to wait until later, because she needed to get ready for work.

Whenever Chavonne got mad at Leon, she invariably felt hungry. Since, lately, she was mad at him more often than not, it had become practically impossible for her to stick to a diet. It was already hard enough, working at Drip 'n' Donuts, surrounded all day by assorted sticky and sugary pastries that beckoned to her to eat them. While dressing for work, those iced devil's food cake donuts with candy sprinkles already dominated her thoughts. She had to suck in her breath to get her blouse buttoned.

"Damn yo' ass, Leon," she hissed, "for makin' me fat."

"What, huh?"

Chavonne hadn't realized that she was speaking out loud. "Ain't nothin'," she said softly, then left the bedroom. "Go back to sleep."

Fortunately, he complied and resumed snoring.

Chavonne didn't want him to wake up enough to get his brain working, because then he'd start talking his usual bullshit and flattery, which always ended in him asking for money to drive to the employment office, or to make copies of his resume, or pay to have his interview suit dry cleaned, or some other legitimate but unverifiable expense. Most often, even though she knew better, she succumbed to his sweet talk and left him with some walking around money, although less than he asked for just to make a point. He had a way of accepting the cash from her while managing to sound both appreciative yet disappointed at the same time.

At least he didn't know about her tips stash, which she'd hidden behind a panel in the laundry closet. He'd never think to look there, since he'd never, in their five years of living together, washed the clothes—not even once. Those tips were small, as people weren't normally very charitable tippers at the drive-thru. Furthermore, she had to share the proceeds with co-workers, which was a goddamned rip-off, but she couldn't complain about it without getting accused of not being a "team player". Still, all that pocket change added up, and someday she hoped that she'd have a nice sum to spend on something just for herself, and not even tell Leon.

While Chavonne watched the microwave oven count down re-heating a leftover breakfast sandwich, the hip-hop clip on her cell phone — *skrrrrt* — sounded, indicating that she'd just received a text message. That could only mean one thing.

She slapped her finger across the screen to open the text from Wanda Pfaff, that skank.

SYK 2DAY, NO CAN WRK, 2MORO MAB, W :(

Damn that girl's ass!

This marked the third time Wanda had claimed to be sick since the last time Chavonne had taken off a day, and they were supposed to take turns covering each other's backs. Probably that scabby 'ho was in bed with some dick she hooked up with after a night of drinking Hennessy and vanilla Cokes at the Electric Company, where she could always find some dude ready to dive low enough to bang her.

What was worst, though, was that Wanda was supposed to pick her up on the way to work. Now, Chavonne had no choice but to kick Leon's lazy ass out of bed and make him drive her, which meant that she'd have to give him the keys, which meant that he'd keep the car all day, which meant that he was sure to ask for money, which meant that....

Damn those consequences!

She had to stifle her thoughts, because she knew that once they started spinning into a hole, there was no bottom. The best way to cope with Leon was not to think about him. Those devil's food donuts sounded mighty appetizing, right about now.

5:20 AM

The smooth, seductive voice with a slight Latin accent teased Val Vargas with a gentle, "*Buenos dias,* darling."

The voice insinuated itself into a dream in which Val played the music box dancer song, on a grand piano—she could not play the piano, or any musical instrument—center stage at the Ohio Theater. The sound wafted from her soul through her music, rising like a gently swirling summer breeze into the ornate domed ceiling, surrounding her in a euphonic cloud. The voice belonged to a caped, shadowy male figure in the front row, who rose from his seat and beckoned her to "awaken to a new adventure."

Val squinted, squirmed, sighed, rolled over, and reached for the nightstand. Devoid of any conscious thought, she utilized muscle memory in executing a gesture to set the cell phone alarm to snooze, thereby allowing herself another ten minutes of bliss. Then, burying her head in pillow, she drifted effortlessly back to the concert hall and to her mysterious paramour.

5:25 AM

"*¡Ay! Por favor, Tati,*" Ximena Gonsalves insisted, standing in the doorway. "*¡Escucha!*"

"Huh?" Tatiana covered her ears and moaned, acting as though she didn't understand. "Speak English."

"Repeat what I just spoke to you."

"What for? Don't you even listen to yourself when you talk?"

Now she was just being *malévolo* to provoke her. Why, Ximena wondered, did they have to go through such drama every single weekday morning? Why did Tatiana, the eldest child, who was sixteen—old enough to accept some responsibility—instead act as if being persecuted whenever Ximena asked for even the most *minúsculo* of a favor? Would it have killed her, just once, of her own accord, to get out of bed, get dressed, kiss her dear *mamá* goodbye, and promise to take care of everything? Wasn't that what good daughters did?

"I am asking you to repeat the words I just said because I need to be sure you have understood me."

Tatiana "meh"-ed in exasperation, which Ximena assumed was meant to convey that she regarded her mother's request to be patronizing.

Insults she could tolerate, but Ximena didn't have the spare time to deal with outright recalcitrance. She was looking for something to throw at Tatiana—not to hit her, but just to graze her enough to prove that she meant business—when their Manx cat padded into the room to investigate the fuss. Ximena swooped it up and tossed it onto her daughter's bed, where it landed claws first.

Both the cat and the girl snarled indignantly.

"Oh, you did *not* just do that, did you mother?" Tatiana jumped up and down on the bed. "That's child abuse!"

Hands on hips, Ximena commenced interrogation. "After I have left, at 6:15, what is it that you do?"

Tatiana sat on the edge of the bed, mounds of curly hair hanging in front of her face, her shoulders pointing like spears, and she spoke in the deadpan voice of a captive soldier reciting name, rank, and serial number: "Wake up Ick and Booby."

"Yes. You must wake up Ignacio and Barbette. Now, at 6:30, what do you do?"

"Breakfast."

"Yes. I've put the cereal and their bowls at the table. At 6:50?"

"Get dressed."

"Yes. I've laid out clothing for all of you on the dresser. 7:15?"

"Bus stop."

"Yes. And do not forget to text me when they get on the bus."

Tatiana's pent up irritation burst out: "¡Si, Si, Si, Si, Si, Si!" She sighed dramatically. "Really? Give me some credit! Do you think that I'd just put them into a car with some old perv like Mister Moon next door? You really think that I'm such a major fu... *screw* up, don't you, mother?"

Glad for even the smallest sign of respect, Ximena was gratified that Tatiana had stopped herself from saying *fuck*. She felt a fleeting tingle of maternal satisfaction that almost passed for a mother-daughter bonding moment.

"There is one more thing that I'd like for you to do."

Tatiana threw her hands over her head. "Oh, really, like what, huh? What's that? Wash the dishes? Scrub the toilets? Should I clean the litter box before I go to school? How about I should stop at the blood center and give some plasma for extra food money? Do you want me to sell my virgin body to creepy old Mister Moon so that we can pay the mortgage? What'll it be, mother?"

"I was going to say that I would like for you to have a *muy buen día*."

"Oh. Okay then, but...." Tatiana scooted out of bed, shook back her hair, clasped her hands together in front of her, and curled her lower lip into a pouty face. "Do you think you could bring home some of those yummy Boston Cream donuts with the chocolate icing tonight?" A pause for effect.... "Please, *mamá*."

"*Con mucho gusto, princesa*."

If donuts could facilitate even brief harmony in the household, then Ximena refused to care that Tatiana was getting chubby. Hell, she was willing to stuff a baker's dozen donuts into a feedbag and strap it to Tatiana's face, if that kept her happy. Besides, taking home day old pastry was just about the only perk available to her in that otherwise hateful job of hers.

5:30 AM

The mellifluous voice that Val had selected from a sample of hundreds of freely downloadable audio clips spoke again. This time, the voice resonated with increased ardor. "You must rise and shine, dearest. Open your eyes."

In the ten minutes since the first wake-up call, she'd descended to a more physical level of dreaming, where she was aware of her body, but still felt like she was floating, wrapped beneath layers of buoyant blankets with her head supported by multiple pillows, which in her dreams became gently undulating waves.

At the same time, she was also conscious enough to feel the pull of those words, summoning her earthward with gentle insistence. When the voice urged her, again, to "open your eyes," she recoiled, biting the insides of her cheeks and squeezing her eyelids shut tight.

With the same automatic motion as before, she swiped a single finger across the screen of her cell phone, enabling another ten minutes to snooze.

5:38 AM

On nights when Tank Turner went drinking at the Zig Zag Club, he parked his Dodge Ram truck behind the dumpster next to the Dollar Store, across the street from Drip 'n' Donuts. In this way, after closing the bar at 2:00 AM, he could stagger to the truck, climb into the back, catch a couple of hours of boozy sleep, and still get to work on time the next morning. It wasn't as if he could go anywhere, anyway, with that damn breathalyzer hitched to the truck's ignition.

Whenever he slept in his pickup, he supposed that he was still technically drunk when he clocked in at 6:00 AM, but he figured that the old bitch, Ms. Johar, appreciated punctuality over sobriety. So long as he wasn't hurling chunks or shitting squirts, he could soldier through low-grade headache and nausea. It wasn't as if he needed to use any higher cognitive functions just to operate the turbo chef oven. Besides, a moderate hangover helped the day pass faster.

It had been colder than icicles hanging from a polar bear's balls when Tank staggered out of the Zig Zag Club, but when he closed the canopy door behind him, he lit a survival candle and placed it on the wheel well. With that and his heavy-duty sleeping bag, not to mention a high blood alcohol level, he stayed toasty for the duration of the night. In the army, while in Afghanistan, he'd developed a skill for falling asleep immediately and deeply, irrespective of environmental conditions, up to and including submachine gun fire, mortar shells, sand storms, scorching heat, and scorpions crawling over his ass. Without the ability to ignore distant and/ or non-lethal threats, he'd never have gotten any shuteye over there. However, if the outpost's danger siren went off, he could shift gears from dreaming about getting a blowjob from Bashira through the mouth hole in her burqa, to heart pounding, wide awake, on his feet and combat ready in half a second's time. It was a somewhat transferable skill to his current lifestyle, which often left him with minimal turnaround time from sloppy drunk to reporting for duty.

Absent any active combat to awaken him, Tank depended on Huck to rouse him in time for work. Huck had offered to perform that service, no strings attached. Initially, Tank declined, not giving a reason other than to say, "I don't think so."

Still, Huck had insisted, swearing it was no inconvenience because, where Tank parked his truck, it was visible from the sidewalk between the bus stop and Drip 'n' Donuts. If Huck noticed it when he got off the bus in the morning, he'd just bang a couple of times on the aluminum roof of the canopy to let Tank know it was time to get up.

Tank had agreed to the arrangement but remained suspicious, as he always was of favors. Oh, Huck wasn't a bad kid, even though he was a fag, a gook, and commie. The biggest drawback, though, was that Huck was so damn responsible that he usually clocked in for work early, which meant waking Tank up a few minutes before absolutely necessary.

So, when Huck rattled Tank out his stupor by slapping the roof, the first thing Tank did was check his watch for the time—5:38 AM.

Huck kept banging until Tank shouted, "Go away, asshole!" He meant it appreciatively.

The side windows of the canopy were glazed with hoarfrost. Tank melted a peephole by pressing his palm against the window, and looked through it to the grim, urban winter scene. It had started to snow. Under the streetlights, flakes flashed and twinkled in the wind like sparks from a magic wand, but as soon as they blew into the darkness, they lost all form and became swirling streaks, reminiscent of a bad experience he'd once had with hallucinogenic mushrooms. The storefronts in the strip mall sat dark and desolate, except for the lonely Drip 'n' Donuts, which stood out in stark relief against the abyss, with its migraine-inducing fluorescent lights seemingly intensified by the clear glass frontage. Just inside the door stood a silver tinsel Christmas tree, decorated with a blinking garland of multicolor LED lights. Not a soul was visible inside, as if it had been abandoned hastily and nobody turned off the lights.

By contrast, headlights of the slow and already heavier-than-usual traffic on Cleveland Avenue looked blurry through the haze and snowfall. Brake lights flickered on and off repeatedly, and Tank watched a couple of cars spin out while making left turns from Innis Road, where it looked to him like an accident was just waiting to happen. In inclement weather, some folks who worked on The Ohio State University campus, or in downtown Columbus, sometimes drove on Cleveland Avenue to avoid the freeways. Backlogs occurred when the increased traffic mixed with the regulars—security guards and cleaning staff returning from their night jobs at suburban office complexes; single mothers grabbing any excuse for food to serve as their kids' breakfasts before dropping them off at day care; the commuting businesspeople from Clintonville, who regularly cut across Innis Road en-route to jobs at Easton or in New Albany; not to mention the old timers from the neighborhood, who still woke up early out of immutable habit, even though long retired.

In any case, it meant the drive-thru would be extra busy. Something about bad weather seemed to make people crave donuts.

Tank retrieved his Drip 'n' Donuts shirt from on the floor of the pickup's bed, where he'd balled it up and tossed it after peeling it off the previous night. He opened the shirt and shook it in the snow, a half-measure for washing it, hopefully good enough to extract the worst stains and smells. Then he threw back his head and stretched his arms, as if showering in the snow.

Before trudging off to work, he swished some mouthwash, blew his nose, and snuck around behind the dumpster to take a piss. Basic hygiene taken care of, Tank felt good to go for a nine-hour shift.

5:40 AM

With the snooze options having been exhausted, the program on Val's cell phone alarm defaulted from the smooth baritone of her Latin beau to something more imperative. The blast of a French ambulance siren filled the room and savaged Val's eardrums like audio drill bits against her tympanum. The force snapped her eyes open so wide that she felt the skin tighten on the back of her neck. She grimaced and ground her teeth. Her heart beat like a captive beast trying to break through her rib cage.

She clapped her hands over her ears and shrieked, "Oh poop, poop, poop! Why didn't the alarm go off? Now I'm gonna be late for work!"

And she hopped from her bed with alacrity, as if being chased by a guilty conscience.

6:02 AM

Ms. Uma Johar rubbed her temples while listening to Scooter Opalinsky deliver the bad news from the overnight shift.

Scooter said, "The delivery meant for here got unloaded at Polaris by mistake, so you're left with not enough maple bacon donuts, turkey sausage instead of pork, egg white instead of whole eggs, and more smoothie mix than you guys will use in a month. Meanwhile, up there in the suburbs, they'll be wondering what they're going to tell their customers when they run out of veggie scrambler wraps."

She couldn't prove it, but Ms. Johar was certain that, somehow, this mistake was all Scooter's fault. Whenever he mentioned Polaris, it sounded to her like he longed to go back there, where everything was posh and brand new, like the black leather easy chairs in its "lounge," its two-lane drive-thru, and a fancy new, app-driven, online ordering system. He often started his sentences by saying, "Well, when I worked at Polaris...." The Cleveland Avenue shop always suffered by comparison.

Business had been running more-or-less smoothly until three weeks ago, when the erstwhile day manager at the Grove City Drip 'n' Donuts store suffered some kind of mental breakdown. She walked away from her position in the middle of a shift, carrying with her a chocolate frosted donut that she claimed bore the image of the Virgin Mary in its swirls. This event had triggered a chain reaction, whereby the suits at the regional headquarters transferred the night manager at Cleveland Avenue to fill the Grove City vacancy, thereby aggravating the night manager at the latter, who believed himself worthier of the position, to the point where he, too, walked off the job. That had led to an additional transfer of yet another staff position from Cleveland Avenue to Grove City.

To Ms. Johar, the last remaining staff supervisor at Cleveland Avenue, these events confirmed the belief that her store was the poor stepchild of Drip 'n' Donut franchises in the Greater Columbus area, always treated like the lowest priority.

She spent a frantic day on the phone with Mr. Jack Gentile, the regional manager, begging for help. He offered sympathy, urged her to "hang in there," and promised to do "something" as soon as possible.

The "something" that he eventually did was promote Scooter Opalinsky, who had all of three months experience at the Polaris shop in the suburbs north of Columbus, to serve as her interim night manager. Ms. Johar was convinced that Jack Gentile had selected Scooter for the assignment because staff at Polaris wanted to get rid of him. He had freckles and a puppyish quality that she found unseemly for a manager, and although he insisted that his proper name was indeed "Scooter," she simply could not bring herself to speak of him using an epithet that described an ignoble form of locomotion. Still, he was all the help she was likely to get until they could hire new people, and the paperwork was stuck in HR at the regional office, where paperwork often disappeared without a trace. In the meantime, she and Scooter had been working twelve-hour days, five days a week — exempt from overtime, of course — with no relief in sight.

"May I assume, then, that you placed a new order for the afternoon delivery?"

Scooter shrugged. "I figured you ought to do that. I mean, you know what's needed down here better than I do. Am I right?"

On one hand, Ms. Johar felt gratified at Scooter's apparent deference to her authority. On the other hand, she was not so flattered that she did not recognize a cop out. He was right about one thing, though: she had zero confidence in his ability to handle the task, so it was best that he'd left it for her to do.

"I will take charge of this situation," she said.

"Okay, then. Good luck. I'm outta here."

"Please close the door behind you."

With one foot outside the office, Scooter skidded to a stop, turned around, and called back to her. "It looks like your team is awaiting your orders."

She pushed back her desk chair and went to ascertain what the problem was this time.

Standing side-by-side like a picket line in front of her office, the team members of the Drip 'n' Donuts morning crew presented themselves for duty.

Privately, she referred to them as her "dalits." In a single eyeful, she could count about a dozen policy violations, not to mention basic lapses in etiquette and cleanliness, which she made a mental note to cite in their personnel files, but otherwise said nothing.

The dalits sighed as a group.

"What is this matter?" Ms. Johar asked.

Chavonne said, "That Wanda Pfaff done called sick again."

Ximena added, "And Val is late, again."

It irritated Ms. Johar that the team knew very well what she expected of them, but they refused to act until she told them what to do. Their dependency seemed vindictive, like petulant children testing her. Still, summoning her inner brahmin, she spoke, gesturing and pointing at each of them accordingly.

"For now, then, Chavonne, you will perform the duties taking drive-thru orders. Please spit out your gum. Hyun-ki, put on your nametag, and you will have to run orders *and* serve at the pickup window. Ximena, you can handle both front counter positions until Valerie reports for work. Please do not forget to mute your cell phone. And, of course, Mr. Turner— tuck in your shirt—has the kitchen. Any questions?"

There were none.

Ms. Johar could not understand why none of them moved until she clapped together her hands and said, "Why do you continue looking at me?"

Without another word, she pivoted, marched into her office, and pulled the door shut behind her.

Inside the office, she leaned with her back to the door, rubbed her eyes, bent her knees, and slid down slowly into a squat, wrapping her arms around her legs—a posture like a fetus resisting birth.

"Bitch," Tank mumbled as the door closed behind Ms. Johar, loud enough so that everybody could hear. Nobody disagreed, and he did *not* tuck in his shirt.

CHAPTER 2

6:10 AM

Huck objected to several things about wearing his nametag. First, as a matter of principle, he disapproved of wearing any trademarked corporate logo or brand name. Not even images that were familiar or fondly regarded — like those for bars, beers, cartoon characters, sports teams, rock bands, superheroes, or Brutus Buckeye — were free from the taint of moneyed sponsorship. Huck's antipathy to anything commercial included the Drip 'n' Donuts logo — one D dripping onto a second D, lying on its back — despite his being required to wear its matching cap, shirt, and nametag as a condition of the job. Second, as he'd explained to Ms. Johar numerous times, he did not feel that it was fair or appropriate for front line employees to surrender their identities by displaying nametags on their chests, while managers were not required to similarly reveal themselves. Third, even though his given name was, in fact, Hyun-ki, he was born and bred in rural Knox County Ohio, the corn-fed son of a farmer, and nobody had ever called him that, not even his South Korean mother who'd named him — and who, until he went to college, had been the only person of Asian descent he'd ever met. For all of his life he'd answered only to "Huck."

It was more than just a matter of semantics to him; he'd come to take pride in bearing the name of a populist literary character whose most famous words were, "All right then, I'll go to hell."

As a form of passive protest, when he pinned the nametag to his shirt, he left it loose and crooked, dangling face down, so that if somebody really wanted to read it, they'd have to bend over and tilt their heads as if they were ducking for low clearance.

Chavonne fussed with her headset. "I ain't ne'er gonna git used to wearing this thing," she complained. "It reminds me of when I was a kid and had to wear braces."

Huck realized that this was just her way of sustaining complaints against Wanda Pfaff, who, in the typical distribution of labor, would be taking orders. Actually, he had the biggest grievance against Wanda, because her absence forced him to work two jobs: running orders and managing the pickup window.

"Would you prefer to switch jobs?" he asked.

"Nuh uh, no way!" Chavonne held an empty mayonnaise jar with a post-it pad taped to it, on which she'd written the word "TIPS" in bold marker. She dug into her pockets and unearthed a one dollar bill and some loose change. After counting it, she tossed it into the jar and handed it to Huck.

"I jus' done primed the jar with one buck and sixty-eight cents. So, I want that much back before we divide us up our tips at the end of the shift," she said.

Huck shook the jar and placed it prominently in the window, where customers couldn't miss seeing it. He had mixed feelings about tipping: on one hand, he appreciated the expression of communality, but on the other hand, there were worthier causes deserving of charity. Besides, the underlying issue—the real criminality—was the low wages Drip 'n' Donuts paid its employees. He didn't understand why his colleagues seemed so indifferent when he spoke to them about unionizing.

As he logged into the cash register, a loud sputter and backfire came from the drive thru, prompting him to glance at the fish-eye rear-view mirror.

A ramshackle Volkswagen van appeared out of the gloom and lurched to a stop next the menu kiosk. Foul smoke belched from its exhaust, inking the snow with soot. The driver appeared only as a bent-over male silhouette, with a pointy hood on his head.

Chavonne cleared her throat of her usual slang, then intoned the standard company greeting: "Welcome to Drip 'n' Donuts. How can I make your morning great?"

Huck watched the monitor until the order blinked onto the screen: a bag of fifty donut holes, called "drippies," of special holiday varieties, including 15 snowflake sprinkled, 15 brown sugar cinnamon, 10 red and green jellies, and 10 candy cane frosted, with one large peppermint mocha hot chocolate, extra whipped cream. Gluttonous excess, Huck mused, but undoubtedly festive.

When the van pulled forward under the metal halide street lamps, he could make out its colors and peculiar details. Its body was streaky turquoise, looking as if someone had painted with a thick brush, and it faded to a pale blue on the front and around the wheels. Its roof stood out in bright green, as though moss were growing on it. It had eyebrows sketched over round headlights, a handlebar mustache beneath its circular VW logo, and a crooked smile on the front bumper. What looked to Huck like the patchwork remnants of a Mexican poncho curtained the windows along both sides of the van.

The amply bearded driver wore his frizzy, sterling silver hair in a braided ponytail tucked into his collars, and a red and green bandana tied across his forehead. He was dressed in layers: a twill camouflage jacket over a hooded fleece with a Chief Wahoo logo, over a plaid flannel shirt, unbuttoned, over a fake tuxedo with bow tie t-shirt. He wore fingerless gloves, except for the thumbs, and wire glasses with one lens cracked. His nose hair merged into his mustache, which was spiked with tiny, glistening crumbs of what looked like powdered sugar.

An old hippie, Huck mused, approvingly.

When the man rolled down the van's window, intense vapors of marijuana rolled out like the leading edge of a storm front, making Huck's sinuses tingle and his eyes water. He steadied himself and said, "Whoa..."

The man giggled through his nose. "You got that right, son."

Huck creased the top of the bag full of drippies, handed him the order, and said, "You're loading up on the holiday sweets this morning, huh?"

"I plan to spread some Christmas cheer today."

Meanwhile, behind them in the drive-thru, the next customer, piloting a black Pontiac Bonneville with blinding halogen headlights and a shiny, golden crown on the dashboard, pulled up to the kiosk.

Chavonne took the next order.

"Apropos of that," the old hippie continued. "Here is a twenty dollar bill. By my calculations, my order comes to fourteen dollars and some odd change. Please, take the rest and use it to pay for a donut and cup of coffee for the next person in line."

"Why, yes, sir. Thank you. Pay-it-forward, eh?"

The old hippie wrapped his arms around his chest, as if trying to hold something inside, before breaking into a hearty, bowel-shaking guffaw — *har-dee-ho-ho* — over and over. Finally, he regained his composure and said, "I do hope so."

Then he drove away, the van's rear end sliding slightly on a patch of ice when it turned onto Cleveland Avenue.

That transaction complete, Huck turned his attention to the monitor and went to grab the next order: one apple fritter and a large cappuccino, extra sugar. He bagged it and waited, looking forward to telling the customer about the kind soul who'd pre-paid for his order. It wasn't often that he got to deliver good news.

The black Pontiac pulled next to the pickup window. The driver wore goliath glasses, a pork pie hat, a white fur-trimmed jacket, and had a gold-capped front tooth. His silver bracelets jangled and his platinum pinky ring glinted as he took the order from Huck.

"That'd be how much?" he asked.

"There is no charge. The gentleman in the car just ahead of you has already paid for your order."

The man lowered his glasses and locked eyes with Huck. "You're shittin' me, right?"

"Nope. It's true."

"Well, ain't that some shit," the man said. He looked over his shoulder at the Nissan 370Z pulling up behind him, and at the woman driver who stared at herself in the rear-view mirror while applying lipstick. He then handed Huck a ten dollar bill and said, "Yo yo yo, then. Use this to pay for whatever that fine young woman behind me orders. It's like, one good turn deserves anotha'. Ain't that so?"

The man extended his hand, and they sealed the deal with a dap handshake.

Huck held the ten dollar bill by its top corners, stretching it between his thumbs and index fingers, as if he didn't want to fold or soil it in any way. He heard Chavonne greeting the next customer, watched the order appear on his monitor, and paused to consider how the services he was facilitating constituted genuine random acts of kindness.

If only human commerce always worked like this!

Then, maybe society wouldn't be plagued by such debased and dysfunctional corporate tyranny. If only people, united by their compassion and common humanity, shared what they possessed and took only what they needed, always leaving something behind for the next person, then maybe society would be driven by love, rather than greed.

Yeah. Sure.

If only....

CHAPTER 3

7:10 AM

. Adam Erb liked bringing donuts to meetings. Any kind of meeting would do—shareholder meetings, board meetings, executive meetings, team meetings, social meetings, even one-on-one meetings with individual clients. It didn't matter if the meeting was to share information, solve problems, make decisions, or just for the sake of meeting. Hell, he'd been known to offer a donut to employees as a prelude to firing them. No matter what the agenda, Adam believed that any meeting worth attending was, ultimately, a meeting by, for, and/or about him, and bringing donuts was his way of laying claim to it. Otherwise, why would he waste his time being there?

Donuts made a statement for and about him. He designed every step in the process of acquiring, selecting, presenting, describing, sharing, and devouring the donuts to exploit specific strategic objectives. First, he purposefully and self-consciously brought *donuts*—not fancy choux pastries like profiteroles; no flaky desserts like baklava; no braided Danish with cream cheese and strawberries; no chocolate croissants or *anything* French; no grainy bagels or flatbreads with fruity, veggie, or herbal varieties of spreads. No, Adam provided real American donuts, deep fried from flour dough and topped or filled with sweet confectionary supplements. Usually, they had holes, which was also subtly symbolic.

Donuts may have been an indulgence, but they also evoked a workmanlike quality, which is how he chose to present himself. Though he wore a Brioni suit and a Rolex watch, he also sported a perpetual three-day beard and wore a round-headed Brutus Buckeye lapel pin on his jacket, the same pin he'd seen on backpacks and floppy hats around town. He used donuts as an icebreaker and offering, but also to supply a bounty, making him one up on everybody who brought nothing. Even if just an ad hoc or ex officio guest at a meeting, by bringing donuts, he took a degree of ownership over the proceedings.

Somebody would always gasp "ooooh," pleased and excited by the offering, while somebody else would whimper "aaaah," assailed by guilty temptation. Adam excused the eager and relieved the ambivalent by taking the first donut, his favorite powdered sugar, and he'd grin with confectionary flakes smeared over his lips and in the corners of his mouth. By doing this, he expressed his folksiness, but also his bravado. It took a man with supreme confidence and a debonair nonchalance to smile while at the same time wearing a powdered sugar mustache. This simple gesture modeled the tone of the meeting and matched it to his personality, each of which played to his advantage.

Adam even liked personally choosing the donuts. He could have had Jerold or Jerome—whatever his driver's name was—pick them up on his way to work, but ever since they'd opened that gleaming new Drip 'n' Donuts shop at the Polaris suburban mall complex, Adam looked forward to the joys and rewards of the drive-thru. Picking up the donuts enabled him to mix with and by seen by admirers, all without getting out of his car.

From an upstairs window, he watched the Hummer limo as it approached from the long driveway, five minutes early for a 7:15 AM pickup. The new driver—what *was* his name, anyway?—was commendably punctual, even if he did look slightly unkempt, as if he'd slept in his chauffeur's uniform. Adam couldn't decide if the driver sported this ruffled look carelessly or as a conscious style choice, and if the latter, he wondered further what kind of image it portrayed and, more to the point, if he approved of it. Either way, he didn't appreciate having to invest time and mental energy wondering about the intentions of his hired help. Once they punched the clock, they weren't supposed to have any.

He descended the spiral staircase into the foyer and took a route through the kitchen, where he handed his half-empty coffee cup to the housekeeper with instructions for a refill. He continued down the hallway to the sun room, where the nurse was feeding some kind of grayish mush to his old man.

"Bye, Dad," he said, lifting his father's limp hand and giving it a squeeze. Anticipating what would happen next, Adam hopped aside just in time to dodge the old man's projectile spitting of a mouthful of mush.

"Missed me," he jested.

The old man belched.

Adam stepped outside onto the patio just as the driver hustled around the front of the limo to open the door for him.

"Good morning, sir," the driver said.

"Good morning, Jerry."

"Uh, sir, that's Jay-Rome."

"Sorry, Jerome."

"No. that's *Jay*-Rome."

"Donuts," was all Adam said to him.

By speaking that one word, he conveyed to Jay-Rome that he wanted him to take a detour on the way downtown, stopping at Drip 'n' Donuts. En route, Adam sprawled in the back, sipping a Red Bull and inspecting the Drip 'n' Donuts menu on his cell phone. He made it a point to know precisely what he wanted to order and to speak first when the limo reached the drive-thru, before the greeter had a chance to utter, "Welcome to Drip 'n' Donuts...." He looked forward to the expressions on the staff members' faces when he lowered the tinted window in the back of the limo and greeted them with his trademark wink and index finger salute.

When they arrived at Polaris, Jay-Rome pulled the limo forward so that Adam's window was directly across from the speaker on the ordering kiosk. Adam took pride in articulating clearly, so that he never had to repeat.

"Felicitations," he said. "I would like to order a dozen donuts, two each: glazed, old fashioned, chocolate frosted, Boston cream, cinnamon, and powdered sugar."

Upon finishing, he waved Jay-Rome forward to the next window. The cashier, who had a jade nose ring, stopped herself in the middle of repeating the order. When she glimpsed Adam, her jaw dropped so far that the mouthpiece on her headset slid straight down, as if pointing at her cleavage.

"You're... *you!*"

"Adam Erb at your service."

"Oh-my-god!" She smoothed back her hair and licked her lips. Her name tag read *Phoebe*. "I am like your very hugest fan."

He tilted his head slightly sideways, but with an angled half-smile and eyes looking upward, the very pose that he'd donned for the cover of last month's *Columbus Magazine*, the one in which he'd been declared the state of Ohio's most eligible bachelor.

Phoebe leaned forward and half-whispered to him, "I'm wearing a pair of Skivvies right now...."

It used to dumbfound Adam when women that he didn't know spoke to him candidly about their intimate apparel. Now, he'd have been surprised if they didn't.

"I hope they're treating you right. Yes?"

She blushed, giggled, and gasped. *"Oh, yes."*

Adam caught Jay-Rome glance back at him in the rear-view mirror and shake his head. Of course, guys like Jay-Rome didn't get it, or just wished that they could. Watching Adam work his charm... what else could they do but shake their heads?

Sometimes, Adam didn't quite get it himself — how a dumb idea that he'd dreamed up while in business school had taken off like a screaming rage, gone viral in a heartbeat, accumulating memes, momentum, and mountains of profits, which formed the foundation of his burgeoning business empire. He called the prototype garment "Drawers," and sold them as boxer shorts with a patented "whisper zip" Velcro waistband and fly, and, inside, a mesh testicle holster. Who knew that men were so hungry for accessorized undershorts? That success had led to the ravenously popular line of feminine intimate garments, called "Skivvies," which utilized real velvet Velcro, not the polyester crap used on baseball caps. Its straps separated with an alluring *pffft* and, reportedly, tickled in all the right places. There seemed no limit to what one could accomplish with lace, sheer fabrics, strips of high-end Velcro, and assorted forms of costume jewelry and other ornamentations. His latest innovation was an edible line of products.

Buoyed and financed by the success of his underwear enterprise, he'd then purchased vacant buildings in suburban strip malls across town, and re-branded them as a chain of public bathhouses and saunas called "Tubs of Fun," which attracted millennials as a date night alternative to the club scene. Some of the more popular locations required reservations months in advance.

As his next investment, Adam acquired majority ownership of the local professional women's roller derby team, which he re-named the Cow Town Milk Maids, and made a killing selling gear and residuals. Finally, acceding to the popular demand of his Twitter followers, he launched a whole new career as a blogger, podcaster, public speaker, and dispenser of advice on subjects concerning relationships in the twenty first century.

Nothing that Adam tried in his adult life had resulted in anything less than tumultuous success. He found it hard to understand, but easy to take for granted, and the reason America was the greatest country on Earth, ever.

While waiting, Jay-Rome whistled through his teeth.

This irritated Adam slightly, for it seemed too casual, even tacitly disrespectful. It occurred to him that, maybe, he ought to fire Jay-Rome, just for shits and giggles. Not now, though—at least not until he got where he needed to go.

"Is that him?" somebody called from inside the store.

"Let me see." A second young woman—Pandora, according to her name tag—went to the window to catch a glimpse, and shouted, "Hey, everybody, you gotta see this!"

En masse, every employee in the donut shop gathered around the drive-thru window.

Lastly, trailing behind the others, a puzzled but curious middle-aged woman with streaks of chartreuse in her hair, wearing wide, floral acetate eyeglasses, approached. "What's going on here?" she asked?

"It's Adam Erb, Ms. Doody!"

"Oh, the underwear guy?"

Ignoring Ms. Doody, Phoebe asked Adam, "Can we get a selfie? Please?"

"It would be my distinct pleasure," he responded, which was how he always responded to that question. He stepped out of the car and framed himself in front of the drive-thru window. Meanwhile, inside the shop, every business transaction ceased so that the entire staff could squeeze into the photo. Adam helped to steady the selfie stick, held up his hand to trigger the shutter, and told everybody to, "Say fritter!"

Upon taking half a dozen shots, Adam unsnapped Phoebe's cell phone from its selfie stick so that he could be the first to see the photos. He deleted those in which he appeared a bit off-center, and others where the dim light shadowed his complexion, ultimately keeping just two. In one of the keepers, he also noticed that beyond the wreath of smiling faces, in the far background of the picture, a cop sat alone at the counter, a donut in front of his open mouth, his expression concealed behind mirror sunglasses. When Adam handed the phone back to Phoebe, he looked, but the cop was gone.

Phoebe scribbled something onto the bag of donuts before giving it to Adam. He took the debit card receipt, signed it after adding a $100 tip, and blew a kiss to Phoebe in parting.

"Boo-yah!" she exclaimed. "Thank you thank you thank you!"

"It has been a joy doing business with you. I'll put in a good word for all of you."

"Thank you thank you thank you! A good word? With who?"

"Mister Jack Gentile."

"The regional manager?" Ms. Doody asked. "You could do that?"

"We're old friends. I'm sure he'll be pleased to learn of your friendly and high quality service."

Adam slid back in his seat and powered up the window, leaving just a crack open in which to call out, while pulling away, "Hashtag... daily donut!"

When he reached into the bag for a powdered sugar donut, he noticed Phoebe's phone number written under the fold at the top. He entered it into a folder on his cell phone and indexed it with three stars.

In the front of the limo, Jay-Rome sighed and shook his head again.

"Do you have something to say to me, Jay-Rome?"

Jay-Rome whistled with admiration. "You sure enough got the world eating out of your hand, Mr. Erb. More power to yah."

On second thought, Adam Erb decided that he would not fire Jay-Rome.

CHAPTER 4

7:20 AM

"Huck, can yo' spell me at the window for a few ticks?" Chavonne asked, handing him the headset. "I gotta go whiz."

It continually amazed Huck how she changed her speech from syrupy to streetwise as soon as she stepped out of her customer service persona. He presumed that by "a few" she intended not only a trip to the restroom, but a cigarette or two on the patio.

"I don't think so," Huck objected. "Why don't you ask Ximena?"

"Nuh uh. I'm askin' yo'."

"I'm kind of overwhelmed trying to keep track of this pay-it-forward chain."

"Say huh? I thought somebody done broke that up already."

"It's been going over an hour, forty customers and counting."

"How's the tips addin' up?"

"Huh? Good, I guess. I'm keeping the pay-it-forward funds entirely separate from the tips." He opened a file on his tablet and showed her the screen. "I made a quick T-account in Excel, so I can monitor charges and surplus payments."

"What's extra ought to go straight into the tips, right?"

Huck hadn't considered that, but it seemed a conflict of interest. "That should be a team decision," he said, then, conceding to his own ambivalence, added, "I guess."

Chavonne handed Huck the headset. "I really gotta go, right now. I won't be but a minute. Yo' can manage all right. Just don't screw nothin' up, 'kay?"

Huck stifled what he was thinking, disappointed with himself for having thought it because it wasn't quite politically correct. He tried to guard against non-pc thoughts, but sometimes they just happened anyway.

Twenty minutes later, Chavonne was still absent, and Huck was busting ass to manage both ends of the drive-thru as rush hour continued unabated. Drip 'n' Donuts fronted Cleveland Avenue, near the entrance to a 1960's strip mall, and the drive-thru lane started just past a treacherous speed bump. In heavy business, if more than four or five cars were in the queue, the backup sometimes spilled onto the inner lane of the street. Delays and sudden stops resulted, which invariably triggered frustration, impatience, rude gesturing, and the honks and counter-honking of horns. He worried that paying-it-forward could not survive an outbreak of road rage, and considered asking Ximena for help, but didn't want to reignite an ongoing feud between her and Chavonne concerning which one of them took the most and longest breaks.

So, normally a fast worker, Huck kicked up his pace another notch. Fortunately, the headset had a long cord, and he discovered that, so long as he was careful not to get it tangled, it stretched far enough to take orders and fill them at the same time.

"Good morning, welcome to Drip 'n' Donuts," he chirped into the mouthpiece. It wasn't often that he worked taking orders. Under these circumstances, he kind of liked being the first point of human contact, the bearer of good news. "This is your lucky day," he proclaimed to the arriving customer.

"My *lucky* day? Right." The woman's voice sounded slightly irritated. "Just give me two jelly donuts and coffee with milk and sugar. How much will that cost?"

"Not a cent, ma'am. The previous customer paid for your order."

"Really? I don't get it."

"It's karma, cause and effect, one good turn, reap what you sow, et cetera. We've got a pay-it-forward streak going."

"A random act of kindness?"

"Exactly."

"That's so sweet."

When she pulled up to the pickup window, the erstwhile irritated woman was beaming as if she'd just opened the door to find a surprise party waiting for her.

"Thank you very much," she said as she accepted the bag from Huck. Then, she put a rolled up a ten dollar bill into the tip jar, and pulled away, not another word.

"Whoa!" Huck called to her, but the car turned the corner and was gone.

Dumbfounded, Huck leaned his whole upper body out the window, hoping that she'd stop, back up, and set things right. It couldn't just end like that. She must've made a mistake. Obviously, she'd intended the ten dollars that she'd given as a tip to be used instead to sustain the pay-it-forward streak. At least that was how Huck rationalized it when he removed the cash from the jar and applied it toward the next customer's purchase.

"Amazing," Chavonne remarked when she finally returned. "I figured for sure that this streak thingy would be done by now."

"Nobody wants to be the person who breaks the goodwill chain," Huck said with assurance.

7:45 AM

Car after car came through, occupied by solitary drivers. Typically, the morning stop at Drip 'n Donuts served as some busy person's on-the-run excuse for breakfast, and most orders were a variation on the staples of a caloric pastry and a caffeinated beverage. Everybody had one thing in common, though: they were all in a hurry. Normally, the operation ran efficiently and traffic flowed smoothly, although it could be a fragile equilibrium, subject to breakdown with the slightest interruption. Disturbance in the flow could engender a domino effect of delays and annoyances. That made it all the more peculiar and surprising, then, that in the current pay-it-forward environment, where every transaction took a bit longer due to the additional explanations and decisions required, patience seemed to have broken out.

Chavonne didn't trust it.

A Mazda CX-5 containing four car-poolers wearing identical, business-professional jackets pulled into the drive-thru. Chavonne watched in the fish-eye mirror at their four mouths moving all at once, as the car pulled alongside the kiosk.

"Welcome to Drip 'n' Donuts. How can I make your morning great?"

After several seconds of continued chattering, a woman shouted into the intercom, "I think we've got it. First, the drinks: two large coffees, one black, one cream with double sugar, one cappuccino with extra whipped cream, and one iced caramel latte. Next, the food: one cream donut, one sugar raised donut, one apple fritter, one Belgian waffle breakfast sandwich. To go."

Chavonne rolled her eyes. *Of course, it's to go. This is a fuckin' drive-thru! I swear, sometimes people get stupider when they enter a drive-thru.*

She repeated their order, adding, as she had started doing ever since coming back from her break, "And by the way, today, thanks to the person in line just before you, one donut and one cup of coffee are already paid for."

"Say what?" the driver asked.

Chavonne explained the dynamics of the pay-it-forward process, about how it had started spontaneously and been going continuously for nearly two hours. "It's like... contagious."

A voice from the backseat piped, "Whoa!"

Another said, "Cool!"

An unintelligible dispute then ensued among the car's occupants. Chavonne listened to the chatter and watched in the fish-eye mirror while they discussed. At length, the driver made a palms-down gesture, and each of the other persons in the car leaned forward, looking at the intercom, as if eager to bear witness.

The driver's voice now assumed a sing-songy cadence. "We're all chipping ten bucks to extend the pay-it-forward chain. We'd like to buy one Belgian waffle breakfast sandwich for each vehicle behind us, until the total is spent. Tell them it's from the gang at Eagle Real Estate. Can you do that?"

Chavonne turned to Huck and pantomimed sticking her finger down her throat, before replying, "I think so."

As soon as the car pulled away, she asked Huck, "Can we really do that?"

"That is a dilemma," he said, without really answering her.

"I ain't gonna be the one to tell Tank he's gotta make all of them Belgians!"

Nobody wanted to mess with Tank. The sandwich maker, with his greasy ponytail stuffed under a hairnet and a scraggly beard escaping from the corners of a gossamer face mask, looked like a Viking warrior prepped for surgery. Chavonne suspected that, on his own time, he wore a white robe and mask.

Huck wasn't listening to her, though. His eyelashes fluttered, as if consulting his inner moral code. "I don't think we should accept corporate endorsements," he finally said.

By the time the Mazda had pulled up to the pay window, he'd squared his shoulders and stiffened his jaw, looking as though he knew exactly what to do.

"Let me handle this," he said to Chavonne, and then slid open the window to greet the gang from Eagle Real Estate.

Released from any further responsibility, Chavonne took the next order. This time, though, she neglected to inform the customer of the pay-it-forward streak in progress. Maybe, she thought, this would be the end of it, and people would go back to their usual bitching and moaning, which, in a way, would be kind of a relief.

She couldn't quite make out what Huck was saying, but she could tell from his tone of voice that he'd entered into his lecture mode. He used it when engaging in any discussion about art, politics, economics, current events, popular culture, climate change, or the obscene costs of higher education. The exchange went back and forth for several minutes, which felt like the equivalent of a decade in the lifespan of the drive-thru, before Huck took their money, thanked them, wished them "happy holidays," and then wiped his hands together, as if signaling a job well done.

"Well? What's the dish?" Chavonne asked.

"Each person agreed to contribute one food item and one beverage item for each of the next four customers. They agreed there would be no quid pro quo?"

"No quiddle what?"

"We will not acknowledge them or their employer for contributing to the cause."

"Yo' sure that was copasetic?" Chavonne asked.

"It's the right thing to do. Still, I think it's time we let Ms. Johar know what's going on."

8:00 AM

As much as the corporate entity of Drip 'n' Donuts governed its independent franchisees by clear, established, centralized policies, Ms. Uma Johar knew of none that applied to this particular situation. When Huck brought it to her attention that a perplexing pattern of behavior called "pay-it-forward" had spontaneously emerged from the normal daily hubbub of the drive-thru, her first thought was that she wanted it to end. She was inclined to order Huck to terminate the procession immediately, for she believed all potential problems ought to be nipped in the bud. Still, he'd reported it as if it were good news, and he seemed proud of it. This made Ms. Johar wonder if, indeed, some benefits might come of this pay-it-forward phenomenon. If so, she wanted to take credit for it.

Ms. Johar bought herself time to think by explaining that she would check the pertinent manuals for the any appropriate standard operating procedures. However, after paging through several handbooks and administrative documents, then doing online searches on "pay-it-forward" in the Drip 'n' Donuts franchise managers' intranet site, she concluded that nothing in the entire literature would supply her with any practical guidance.

She drummed her fingers on the desk. Even from the sanctuary of her office, with its partially closed door, she could feel the air rushing by while the staff outside hustled to keep up with business.

Tank complained loudly enough for her to hear. "Hold yer horses, Huck! I can only push out these damn Belgians so fast!"

The way Tank seemed to have projected his voice toward her office made Ms. Johar suspect he'd intended for her to hear those remarks.

It appeared that simply hoping for the pay-it-forward to die of natural causes would not work, so she pushed back from her desk and went to the pickup window. She lingered there, turning her head from side to side to follow the workflow, and tried to seem concerned as she gazed over Huck's shoulder into the fish-eye mirror at the corner.

A succession of cars had lined up, no end in sight.

"What is the current situation?" she asked Huck.

"We have a total of seventy-one consecutive streakers who have paid-forward for the next person in line."

"Steakers? Oh my. Do you mean they are unclothed?"

"No, Ms. Johar, that's just what I call them. We're working on a *streak*. Get it?"

"Why are they doing this? Do they think this is some kind of karma?"

"I don't know. It's about sharing. People want to do it."

"How are you able to keep track of payments amid such mayhem?"

"I have the finances all worked out in a nifty little spreadsheet." He opened an app on his tablet and showed her. "It's a kind of escrow account. Right now, we're running a total credit of $42.50."

"This is not good. Is it?"

"A lot of people have been overspending, or underspending, depending on how you look at it. Some don't use the full amount paid-forward for them. For example, the first customer may pay-forward a Belgian Waffle Sandwich, costing $1.75, but the next person substitutes a jelly donut, instead, which only costs 60 cents. So there's a net difference of $1.10."

"What happens with these surplus funds?"

"I'm keeping track of everything."

"It goes in the tip jar!" Chavonne interjected.

Ms. Johar shook her head. "This will never withstand an audit."

"We need help!" Chavonne blurted out. "We can't keep up!"

Ms. Johar crossed her arms and decreed, "I am going to call the regional manager for advice and guidance. In the meantime, Huck, please tell Ximena that she is relieved of front counter duties and should be of assistance at the drive-thru, until such time as this situation is resolved."

"Ximena! How come not Val?" Chavonne complained, forgetting to cover the mouthpiece on her headset.

"Hello?" a timid voice inquired through the speakers. "I'd like to order two Belgian Waffle Sandwiches?"

Ms. Johar concluded by saying, "If needed, I will be in my office."

8:15 AM

With six months more service than the next most senior customer services associate on the early shift, Ximena Gonsalves had expressed her explicit desire never again to work taking orders at the drive-thru. She'd paid her dues, over two full years of weekday morning rush hours listening to the snarls, sputters, grumbles, and grunts that came out of people's mouths when they voiced their orders into the intercom speaker. It had been a daily struggle to summon a cheerful voice and deliver the line, "Welcome to Drip 'n' Donuts," when taking orders from the ceaseless parade of bitter commuters, strung-out sugar addicts, dead-tired shift workers, overstressed students, road-weary travelers, and harried parents with cars full of whining children. Maybe, in their normal lives, with their friends, families, and loved ones, they were decent folks, but for the ninety seconds they interacted with her, they were mostly assholes. She didn't know and didn't care whether Ms. Johar finally reassigned her to work the front counter as a reward for her longevity, or just so that she'd stop complaining. All she cared about was being *terminado* with working the drive-thru.

"Ain't no freakin' way!" Ximena cried when Huck told her that, per Ms. Johar's instructions, she had to help out at the pickup window.

"We need you," he pleaded.

"Why me? Why not her?" Ximena argued, pointing at Val, who, with her back turned to the counter at that moment, reached for a donut hole, popped it into her mouth, and licked her fingers.

Huck shrugged as if the answer was obvious.

"I need to take this up with Johar."

"Please. I wouldn't ask, but today something special is happening. Don't you want to be a part of it?"

"*Mierda!* Huck, I will do this as a favor just for you." She put one hand on his shoulder, and with the other pulled on his shirt where he'd stapled the flaps together. "Look what you have done. I have a sewing kit in my purse. On your break, take off your shirt and I will fix this button for you."

"You're the best, Ximena."

When she went with Huck to the drive-thru, though, Chavonne headed to cut them off, and immediately removed her headset and tried to foist it into Ximena's hands.

Pushing back, Ximena wagged her fingers and said, "Nuh uh."

Chavonne argued that she'd been wearing the headset all morning and it was somebody else's turn.

Ximena countered that Chavonne could, "Kiss my ass," which prompted Chavonne to call Ximena a "bitch," and Ximena then to flip her middle finger.

At that point, Huck grabbed the headset and, as if to show both of them how it is done, greeted the next customer like a long lost friend. "Welcome to Drip n' Donuts. How can I make your morning great?"

9:05 AM

Huck tried to time it so that he could pick up a sandwich order just as Tank finished it. That way, he could grab and go, with no need to exchange words. Speaking to Tank always ran the risk that Huck would say something wrong, which tended to happen whenever Huck expressed opinions that contradicted Tank's anecdotal experience.

Tank's refusal to be enlightened frustrated Huck. Why, he wondered, were the salt-of-the-Earth working men, who had the most to gain from a more just and compassionate socialist society, always the ones who railed against it most stridently? It was as if they didn't *want* to be enlightened. However, as the morning rush continued unabated after it would normally have begun to peter out, Tank got backlogged and Huck had to pitch in and help. Speaking to him was unavoidable.

"This pay-it-forward stuff ain't nothing but *bowl sheet*," Tank screeched while watching the numbers count down on the Turbo Chef oven. "Ain't nobody really paying no more than what they was goin' t' pay, anyway. They just pay for the next person's, 'stead of their own."

"Yes, but...." Huck had already addressed this objection in his own mind. "It sets a precedent for doing good deeds. The social capital comes not from giving, but from sharing."

"What good does good deeds do, really?"

"Hmmm. That's an interesting question. The underlying concept is that doing something kind for a stranger, with no expectation of anything in return, is contagious. By doing good deeds just for the sake of doing them, you create an example that others will recognize as good, and they will naturally want to reciprocate. When people realize that they are stronger together, nobody will get left behind."

"Really? Is that what you think?" Tank squinted, which caused the hair net to slip over his entire forehead. "That sounds like some kind o' la-de-da liberal fantasy."

"I'm not the only one who believes it. Just look at what's happening—"

"What's happenin' is that my head hurts and I'm sweatin' like a hog!"

He was moist, true enough, but not with the kind of sweat that comes from hard work, but rather the pungent kind that leaks from a body struggling to remove toxins.

Huck added, "Thoreau said, 'Goodness is the only investment that never fails.'"

"Ha! Y'know what I got half a mind to do, Huck? I ought to take my break and go get my truck, buzz right on to the drive-thru, take whatever the person ahead of me already paid for, and cut straight out, leavin' nothin' behind for the next person. That'll put an end to all of them phony good deeds."

The oven's electronic beeper sounded when the display counted down to zero. Huck didn't budge.

Tank huffed. "Fuck all, dude, I'm just jerkin' yer chain. Don't look like I just ran over your puppy."

10:00 AM

Normally, by mid-morning, the drive-thru business had subsided to the point where one person could handle it. This was no normal morning.

Word had somehow gotten out about the pay-it-forward streak, and it had attracted a disparate group of eager, curious, quixotic, faddish, suspicious, and conspiratorial folks, all wanting to see it for themselves. The chain entering the drive-thru continued with a steady queue of five or six vehicles, sometimes as many as eight, so that cars turning into the strip mall from southbound on Cleveland Avenue got stuck in traffic, blocked by the backlog waiting to get into line.

Passers-through asked questions like, "Who's idea was this?" "What's the catch?" or, "Can I get a rain check?"

They made comments like, "Power to the people!" "One thing leads to another," and, "No good deed goes unpunished."

The left saying things like, "Peace out!" "Keep it Real!" "Laissez les bonne temps roulez," or singing, "Happy trails to you, until we meet again...."

Every half hour or so, Ms. Johar came out of her office and asked Huck for a status report. As of the most recent update, they'd served 128 customers, and the overage paid-forward had accumulated to $74.75.

"Tha's all tips, ev'ry red cent," Chavonne insisted.

"How will this end?" Ms. Johar wondered aloud.

10:10 AM

Val felt as though she was missing out on the party. Apart from one cop wearing a Kevlar jacket and seated at a corner of the counter sipping black coffee, in-store business had been non-existent. On front counter duty, she watched the entire drive-thru parade from a distance that seemed to alienate her. She'd offered to help, to which Huck replied, ironically, "Thanks but we're too busy."

So, with absolutely nothing else to do, she concealed her cell phone behind a napkin dispenser and scrolled through her various social media accounts, leaving breadcrumbs in each venue.

All at once, she exclaimed loudly enough to make sure Ms. Johar would hear inside of her office, "Oh my gawd! We are *trending!*"

Ms. Johar came, not bothering to reprimand Val for violating store policy against cell phone usage. "What does this mean?"

"I started it!" Val squealed, her breasts bouncing and stretching her shirt so that the tops of her chest tattoos showed under her collarbones. "Earlier this morning, I tweeted it.

Instant karma! Pay-it-forward @ N. Cols
D&D. Share sum Xmas <3 #Feedthedeed

"I sent it to all my followers, asking them to re-tweet, and I geo-tagged, updated, replied, sent photos to Instagram, Snapchat... and now, look! She thrust her cell phone in Ms. Johar's face. "We're currently number three on Trendsmap for Columbus."

Ms. Johar took Val's cell phone and scanned the various comments and tweeted threads. "Can you make this stop?"

Val raved, "Now it's bigger than any of us!"

CHAPTER 5

10:20 AM

Other than to bring the donuts, lead the introductions, thank everybody for coming, and sit at the head of the table with his cell phone in one hand and doodling with the other, Adam Erb served no genuine purpose at that meeting. He was an idea-man, content to leave the minutiae and negotiations to others with more patience. The details of success bored him. Despite every lecture his old man had given him over the years, money might just as well have grown on trees. In fact, pre-order revenue for his new, embroidered fig-leaf line of thong Skivvies had already exceeded seven figures, or roughly two hundred times City of Columbus's annual budget for emergency 911 services.

It was almost immoral, getting so rich with so little effort.

This present meeting was to discuss his company's desire to acquire licensing rights from the National Football League, to produce a line of Drawers brand undergarments emblazoned with team logos, and customized with players' names and numbers on the crotch and rear end, respectively. The profit potential in this entirely untapped niche marked was huge for both sides. Adam had convened this meeting to hash out details related to permissions, patents, and trademarks. He couldn't help but laugh when discussion about underwear pivoted to the legalities of "intellectual property."

Twenty minutes into the meeting, he'd reached the capacity of his useful attention span. Adam prided himself as a "multitasker," which meant he knew what to ignore and when to pay attention. He'd reviewed the documents but skipped the details in the fine print, fain to remain in ignorance of them, and to trust his lawyers to pick them apart. That's what he paid them for, after all. On that point, he agreed with his Old Man, who'd once opined to him that lawyers are "all foreplay and no fuck." Until proceedings got to the subject of royalties — that is, the "fuck" — he remained uninterested.

Adam occupied himself perusing his social media accounts and checking the statuses of his tweets posted to @adam_erblurbs. Earlier that morning, he'd tweeted:

Breakfast w/ stellar crew @ Polaris D&D.
Indulge #dailydonut

He'd then uploaded the drive thru selfie and linked it to the hashtag. Almost immediately, comments to the posting started appearing in the form of such profound remarks as, "Seize the donuts," "Donut ever give up," and, "It ain't indulgence if you're worth it." What his followers lacked in originality, they more than made up in loyalty and enthusiasm. Sometimes, he tweeted nonsense just to test them. Literally any drivel that he tweeted achieved swift rank among the top trending hashtags in the city, sometimes the state, occasionally even beyond. When he'd launched Skivvies, the resulting online buzz brought Reddit to its knees.

Checking Trendsmap Columbus, he was pleased but less than ecstatic to see that his #*dailydonut* tag listed among the morning's five most popular hashtags with over 10,000 tweets. Though not one of his greatest hits, it wasn't bad for a tweeted whim on a cold December morning in the middle of the week.

Most of that morning's trends covered the usual territory: the Buckeyes' bowl game, the crime blotter, the most popular Christmas gifts, reports about a blizzard that was coming... and another particular hashtag, #*feedthedeed*, which originated with @vvargas:

> *Instant karma! Pay-it-forward @ N. Cols*
> *D&D. Share sum Xmas <3 #Feedthedeed*

Since being posted at 9:12 AM, the tweet had been shared, re-tweeted, and/or commented on in increasing numbers and with accelerating frequency. Facebook users were liking it a lot. Many citizens of the online community declared their intention to go, post haste, to the North Columbus Drip 'n' Donuts to do their parts and pay-it-forward, and that they'd tell their friends, too. Some wondered if Santa would be there. Several claimed it was proof that the "Christmas spirit" was alive and well. One person predicted that it was a sure sign of the second coming of Jesus Christ.

Adam Erb was not so sanguine about all that #*feedthedeed* business. Columbus was not big enough for two separate social media trends related to the subject of donuts. Therefore, he surmised that it must inevitably be siphoning popularity away from his thread. This could not stand!

Adam texted Jay-Rome:

Meet me at the Front Street entrance in twenty.

He then pushed back his chair and announced, "Excuse me, but something has come up."

Adam wiggled his extended thumb and pinky finger in a "call me" gesture to his lawyers, and left the room. Outside the door, Adam thought he heard those in the room exhale a collected breath.

One of his lawyers got up and closed the door with a solid click.

Goodbye to you too, assholes.

Outside the building, next to the curb, Jay-Rome waited by the limo. He opened the door for Adam so that he could get into the vehicle without breaking stride.

"Where to, boss?"

"Something curious is happening on the north side. I want to check it out. Do you know where the Drip 'n' Donuts is on Cleveland Avenue?"

"Yessir. That's in the old Linden neighborhood, in that gnarly strip mall. What's it called?"

"The Amos Shopping Plaza. I haven't been there much recently. It's getting pretty rundown now, with a dollar store, a chiropractor, an Afro hair salon, a Somali coffee shop, an auto parts store, a bowling alley, many empty store fronts... and—fun fact!—the original Drip 'n' Donuts in all of Columbus, still in business, apparently."

"Really? Sounds like you know what's where thereabouts."

"Oh, I do indeed. I lived in an old house on Gerbert Road until I was ten, when my parents divorced. Mom and me moved in with my stepfather,

Mr. Wessler, on his estate in New Albany. My old man stayed in our house, insisting he'd been born there, and would only leave in a box. Dad, he's stubborn. He'd still be living in that dump today, if not for the stroke he suffered last year. I was glad to take him in. Besides, I got a tax break when I unloaded that property on the city, which turned it into an extension of Pumphrey Park."

"Say what! I didn't know that you're from the hood, Mr. Erb."

Something in the chummy familiarity of Jay-Rome's tone irked Adam. He opened his mouth to speak, but unsure what to say, he coughed, which loosened something in the back of his throat. Adam rolled down the Hummer's window, braced his chin against the top edge of the tinted glass, and hacked out a mucid substance across a lane of traffic and onto the windshield of a Kia Sorrento.

"You okay back there, boss?"

Something popped between Adam's ears when he'd spat out the loogie, making room for memories to flood into his mind. He shook them away, fortified himself with a slug of Red Bull, and said, "Just drive, Jay-Rome, and keep your comments to yourself."

CHAPTER 6

10:50 AM

Huck had been keeping a list, just as he always did. An inveterate list-maker, he tracked everything from his annual resolutions, to his daily to-dos, to his "if I won the lottery" wish list. He intuitively organized his mental space into categories, timelines, and if/then flowcharts. Normally, he kept his lists private, for he worried they might be seen as evidence of conventional, even conservative — *gasp!* — habits. Edgar, his cohort at Occupy Columbus, teased Huck that he was "anal," but with Edgar, everything was a double entendre.

At work, though, this skill was an asset that Ms. Johar appreciated, and to which his coworkers deferred, because none of them were any good whatsoever at making lists, much less sticking to them. Never had his list-making skill been more useful than on that day.

It was getting close to lunch, and Huck hadn't taken a single break since he'd clocked in at 6:00 AM. He'd gotten caught up in the momentum of the pay-it-forward experience, and like a gambler running a hot streak, he didn't want to walk away from it. Also, because he'd accepted every forward payment since the beginning of the streak, he'd worked out a bookkeeping system he didn't trust anybody else to maintain. As different cases and circumstances had come up, he'd written on-the-fly rules for handling them on the back of a donut box, and tacked it to the corkboard above the pickup window. Ms. Johar, who had received no instructions whatsoever from regional headquarters, had gladly delegated the task to him, but he wasn't going to be able to hold out much longer without breaking, because he'd been stifling a piss for over an hour. In more ways than one, he needed relief, and right away.

He gestured for Ximena's attention. "Can you cover me for a few minutes?"

"*Dios mio, amigo.* You have not taken a break yet, no? Please, take ten.... No, take twenty.... No, take thirty minutes and go have your lunch. I'll take care of your work station."

"I know. I trust you, but it can get complicated. That's why I wrote down these rules."

"What's these? Let me see.... Ximena took some cheap reading glasses out of her pocket and put them on her nose. "Rule Number One: each customer must pay for at least one item on the menu, in advance, for the next customer in line."

She snapped her fingers. "Of course. That is so simple."

Huck shook his head. "It is, but it isn't. For example, they cannot buy just one donut hole, because we do not sell them by fewer than half a dozen. One cheapskate actually tried to do that. The least expensive item on the menu is one plain cake donut, 50 cents. That's the minimum required to keep the chain intact. However—"

"There's more? Make it easy for me, *por favor.*"

"This is important. The payment forward is for a value, not an item."

"*Que?*"

"If a person pays forward a plain donut for 50 cents to the next person, but that person wants a Belgian Waffle sandwich instead, then the amount of the latter can be reduced by whatever sum was paid forward. So, if I order a Belgian Waffle for $4.25, and the person before me paid in advance for a plain cake donut, what's the difference?"

Ximena waited for an answer, not realizing until Huck made a bouncing gesture with his upturned palms that he was quizzing her.

"Oh," she said. "Let me see then. That is $4.25 for the Belgian Waffle minus 50 cents for the donut, for a total sale of $3.75. *Correcto*?"

"Yes!"

Pleased with herself, Ximena grinned and did a little dance with her shoulders.

"Still, the second person who bought the Belgian Waffles can pay-forward any amount that she wants. Do you understand?

"*Si*."

"Any positive difference between the amount paid forward and the amount actually spent must be recorded here, in an escrow account I created."

"A scarecrow account?"

"Awww."

"I am making a joke. Now go, Huck, before you burst your bladder."

"Okay." Huck took one step toward the restroom, then planted his foot, stopping so abruptly that his bladder sloshed. "Oh! There's one more thing that's very important."

"So many important things! So many rules!"

"I know, but we have to do this the right way. That's why you must understand that maybe the most important rule is that all pay-it-forward transactions are from one person to the next. And they are anonymous."

"Why so is that?"

"This movement is not for flirting or making friends or showing off or buying influence. No. Everybody who participates is equal. There is no charity, no donations, no handouts, and no tax write offs. This is just one person sharing with another, each according to their means and desires. This is for the common good."

Ximena patted Huck on the shoulder. "I will take good care of things. Now, *vamanos* before you start to leak."

10:56 AM

Huck felt relieved to release a long pent-up piss, but also empty and anxious, at a loss for what to do next. He decided to get some fresh air, and stepped outside, where he zipped his coat to the collar and dug his hands through a hole in its pockets and into the lining. Light flurries swirled rather than fell in a cold breeze that wouldn't let go of them. The sky, solid gray and featureless, appeared lower than it had been earlier, having added mass and texture as it sank. It shadowed the horizon and hung like a drooping tent just above the treetops.

Some of the drive-thru customers had informed Huck that a blizzard was coming, He'd often noticed how inclement weather predictably triggered the worst in people, as they fought for and horded what they needed. It made the pay-it-forward streak seem even more precious and fragile.

He stepped gingerly across the icy veneer on the asphalt surface of the parking lot, and walked to the dollar store, where he bought a bag of chocolate-covered raisins and a pack of Winterfresh chewing gum. The line at the checkout extended to four persons long, unusual for the place. The clerk on duty, who typically greeted him with a, "Hey dude," whenever Huck entered the store, was breathing heavily, and sweat glistened across his brow as he hustled to keep up with customers.

"Sure is busy today," Huck commented when his turn came.

"Yeah, I think it's spillover from Drip 'n' Donuts. What's going on over there? Is it some kinda rally or something?"

"You could think of it that way. We have a pay-it-forward streak going—nearly 200 customers, so far. I think of it as the people's Christmas present to themselves."

"Really? Well, here we got our own 'Secret Santa' thing going on, too. All morning, people have been filling our donation boxes like never before, with stuff like toys, school supplies, handkerchiefs, Vaseline, et cetera. Everything we collect goes to the Salvation Army."

Vaseline? Huck wondered. "And you think that it's related to our pay-it-forward at the donut shop?"

"I got no better explanation."

Huck whistled, impressed to think that the magic had spread next door. Before finishing the transaction, he grabbed a box of tissues on display next to the cash register, and added them to the Secret Santa box.

"Merry Christmas, dude," the clerk said.

"And a Happy Festivus to you, too."

Back outside, Huck stepped out from under an overhang and turned his face to the falling snow. He imagined each snowflake to be a crystalized meme, all of them gathering and piling up to create a pristine blanket of hope to cover the world.

He needed to share this feeling, so he swiped the speed dial on his cell phone. "Hey, Edgar, it's me. Yeah, I miss you too, but listen, something is happening at the D&D. Have you heard? No. Well, listen, it's pretty cool...."

That Huck, he is so cute, Ximena thought as she watched him walk across the parking lot, holding his arms out for balance. With all of his rules and accounts, he was so organized, so conscientious, and so responsible—the kind of boy she hoped Tatiana would meet, someday. She wondered how old he was. He looked like a kid, not a trace of facial hair, but she figured him for early twenties. She knew he'd gone to college, then dropped out, complaining that the high price of tuition was immoral because of the greedy banks and the corrupt government.

Or was it the corrupt banks and the greedy government? Never mind. He's probably too old for Tatiana, anyway.

And she did not believe those dumb rumors that he was gay, because she'd noticed him peeking down the blouses of girls in the drive-thru.

Hey, no harm there.

Huck was the kind of boy any mother would want for her daughter.

It doesn't hurt to hope, does it?

11:00 AM

Chavonne didn't fuss when Huck assigned the job of covering the pickup window during his break to Ximena, even though she felt like it should've been her. It would've been fairer to make Ximena work orders and have to wear the headset, for once. On another day, Chavonne might have cried foul and gone straight to Ms. Johar to plea her case, but sometime around mid-morning, without knowing why, Chavonne suddenly realized that the foul and bitchy mood with which she'd started the day had improved, in spite of Leon's shenanigans and Wanda Pfaff's going AWOL. She'd caught a funky Bruno Mars tune in her head, which kept her feet bouncing, and although much busier than usual, she'd gotten into a smooth flow that felt like moon walking.

Customers had been uncharacteristically nice to her, too, calling her "honey," "sweetie," and "sugar." Once, when she greeted a customer with her standard, "How can I make your day great," the voice on the other end of the intercom asked her back, "Do yah feel me, sistah?" She'd purred in response, "Oh yeah. I do feel yah." It felt kind of hot.

And the tips were adding up, too.

Then Leon showed up and ruined everything. She knew it was him before she saw the car, because he honked the damn horn when he pulled up to the kiosk. She'd done told him a hundred times not to do that, so why he kept doing it was a puzzle.

"Hey, Chavonne," he hollered into the intercom before she had a chance to speak.

"Leon! No need to scream. Mind yo'self."

"Ain't you glad to hear me?"

Chavonne pressed the microphone against her lips and said, "Yo' ain't supposed to bother me at work, Leon. How many times I gotta tell yo' that?"

"Oh, well, hey, baby. Anyway, I just wanted my free donut."

"That's why? Leon, don't be no mooch. Them donuts ain't free. Yo' gotta pay-it-forward to the next person."

"But I ain't got no money to spare."

"Yo' damn well better got some money. I done gave yo' twenty dollars in your wallet last night."

A long pause ensued, which made Chavonne anxious, because she knew that whenever Leon sat silent for too long, he was thinking up a lie.

"Never mind," he said.

"Nuh huh. Yo' can't just leave. No matter if yo' like it or not, Leon, this is part of something special, and if yo' break it up, yo' ain't sleepin' in my bed tonight, that's for damn sure."

Ximena at the pickup window, and Tank in the kitchen, stopped their work to listen.

"So listen to me good here now, Leon. Yo' can order whatever, but when yo's done, yo' gotta pay up ahead for the next person. That is to say...." She flipped through the menu looking for the most expensive items. "Yo' gotta pay-forward a giant fruit smoothie with whipped cream and a double Belgian Waffle with bacon."

"But baby, I—"

"Don't argue. Yo's holdin' up the line. I done already placed the order so drive up to the next window to pay. Do it!"

Ximena clapped her hands, and Tank gave Chavonne a big thumbs up.

11:10 AM

"This is hard work," Tank declared, the first words he'd spoken aloud in over two hours.

In Huck's absence, the team had coalesced. With Chavonne taking orders, Val running them, and Ximena working the pickup window, Tank, normally loath to volunteer for anything, agreed to keep an eye on the counter in between filling kitchen orders. This presented no hardship, really, because the counter had remained virtually deserted. The only in-house customer was the strip mall's glib and portly security guard, Bartelby Fusco—nicknamed Flubber—who'd just finished his first of three maple bars when he received orders from a resonant voice over his walkie-talkie to, "Get off your ass and direct traffic."

"Shit," Flubber said.

The dynamics of the drive-thru had become hazardous, as motorists entering it from Cleveland Avenue, and others approaching from one of the two lanes through the mall parking lot, had converged to form a bottleneck at the drive-thru entrance. This had never happened before.

"Wish me luck," Flubber said to Tank as he bagged his remaining maple bars. He tested his whistle to see if it still worked. It did. "I just hope there's not a fight."

"Damn straight fuckin' A," Tank replied.

In Tank's experience, any time too many people accumulated in any one place, trouble inevitably followed. Everybody wound up in somebody's way, or there wasn't enough of something to go around, or one person just didn't like another person's looks, comments, or attitudes. Aggression ensued, the natural response. Sooner or later, somebody in a hurry would cut off somebody else who was in a bad mood, and if either of them had a concealed weapon.... Well, that would put a different spin on the whole pay-it-forward mojo. He was surprised it hadn't happened yet.

Still, whenever Tank stepped out of the kitchen to eavesdrop upon the comings and goings in the queue, and listened to the banter between customers and staff, he was struck by the apparently contagious felicity spreading throughout the whole merry-go-round proceedings. Folks passing through took selfies, videos, or Skyped, and everything wound up on Facebook, Twitter, Instagram, Pinterest, YouTube, or forwarded in texts, emails, Snapchats... and probably still other of those whimsical-sounding social media contrivances that Tank disdained because they were so damn popular. Technology made everybody think they were stars in their own reality shows, and they acted like freaks just to get attention.

Just so, some shady characters had gone through the drive-thru that morning. A woman with neon green hair strummed a ukulele while crooning her order into the intercom. In another car, a Labrador retriever was sitting in the drivers' seat when it pulled up to the pickup window, while its master, working the pedals from the passenger seat, wore a studded dog collar and said, "Arf." One hipster with gasket earrings, dressed in leather and ripped denim, tossed open his jacket, pulled up his shirt, and revealed that he had a Drip 'n' Donuts logo tattooed above his heart.

He kissed Ximena on the lips when she handed him his order, and when he drove off, she was smiling so wide that she needed a second face to contain it.

"Can I work at the window?" Val volunteered.

Tank, in between orders, stared across the counter at traffic backed up on Cleveland Avenue, and saw Olentangy Al, the local panhandler, meander from behind the dumpster across the street. Al pulled his red wagon, as usual, overloaded with twist-tied garbage bags toward Drip 'n' Donuts. The wheel ruts in the snow behind the wagon tracked a digressive route along the sidewalk and across the parking lot, having originated behind a row of vacant storefronts, where, Tank assumed, Al was presently squatting. Most days, Al would stand at the end of the drive-thru holding a scrawled sign on which he'd written "anything helps" onto the back of a donut box, all the while conversing with himself and waving at folks as they passed, smiling at them with teeth so rotten, Tank's fillings hurt just looking at them. He'd stay there for as long as he could, gathering change and the occasional donut from do-gooders, until Flubber showed up and chased him away.

Normally, Tank felt no sympathy for bums, but Al was an armed services veteran, or at least claimed to be, so he belonged in a special category of destitution—those who'd served and then gotten fucked by the government. Tank could relate. Once, he gave Al a six-pack of malt liquor and a ten dollar bill, and told him that, since he already had his booze, he was duty bound to actually spend the cash on food.

"Thanks for understanding," Al had replied, and then started quivering and blubbering, as if it was the kindest thing anybody had ever done for him.

Tank had steadied him with a hand on the shoulder, and said, "Thank you for your service, brother."

Now, Al dragged the wagon behind him like a ball and chain, entering the drive-thru at the point where the queues merged. A black Chevy Silverado truck pulled behind him and kept inching forward, as if to nudge Al out of the way, but he yielded no ground, stomping his feet to assert that he was, in fact, in line for the drive-thru, and not just lost or confused.

"Lookee," Chavonne called to Ximena and Val. "He can't go walkin' through on foot like that, can he? It's a *drive*-thru only, right?"

Ximena scanned Huck's list of rules. "It don't say nothing about walkers here."

Val added, "This guy ain't right in the head."

Chavonne said, "Maybe he's got that *pissed*."

"That's PTSD," Tank corrected her. "And it ain't his fault."

Ximena shook her head. "I feel sorry for him."

Val scrunched up her nose. "It'd be easier to feel sorry for him if he didn't stink so bad."

Tank said, "He's earned the right to stink."

Meanwhile, Al advanced to next in line. He hunched over so close to the intercom speaker that it looked as though he might swallow it, and shouted as if into an echo canyon. "Hello in there!"

Chavonne made a criss-crossing gesture with her arms and said, "Can't we just shoo his ratty ass away?"

Val said, "But that would break the streak!"

Ximena added, "Huck would be *mucho* disappointed if we screw it up while he is on his break."

Tank half sighed, half grunted and, lowering the mesh mask beneath his mouth and beard, marched to the window. "Let me take care of this."

He slid open the window, stuck his head and shoulders outside, and called, "Hey, buddy, come here."

Puzzled, Al slapped at the intercom. "Why ain't this thing damn talkin' to me?"

"That ain't working, but if you come over here, I can help you, brother."

Al pulled the wagon forward and put a hand on the window ledge. "What're you lookin' at?" he asked, pointing over Tank's shoulder to where Val, Chavonne, and Ximena stood ogling.

Tank smiled. "They're looking at a hero, that's what. Where did you serve, brother?"

"Kuwait. Desert Storm. Eleventh Air Defense Artillery Brigade. We kicked some ass over there. We sure did."

"That's what you did, all right." Tank leaned out a bit more. "But here's the deal, just for today. The last person in line has already paid for one donut and a cup of coffee for you. Pick any donut you want, any one at all. What the hell, I'll even upgrade it to a breakfast sandwich, no extra cost, if that's what you want."

"Really? Is this Thanksgiving? I kind of remember it not too long ago, but maybe I'm wrong. What's the catch?"

"Well, to keep things right, you also have to buy something for the next person. See? It doesn't have to be much. Just a plain donut for 50 cents will do. Can you handle that for me?"

"Huh?" Al turned his pockets inside out. "I'm dead busted broke."

"Okay, I figured as much, so here's what you need to do. On the ground under the window, just below the overhang, where the snow hasn't stuck yet, there's almost always some loose change that's fallen into the grass." Tank handed Al a fork. "Here, use this. Look really close and you'll find some money."

On his hands and knees, Al combed the grass and brushed aside snow where it had drifted. "I don't know. Hey, wait. Here's a quarter." He held it up for Tank to see. "Look."

"That's just a nickel, but keep looking. Take your time."

Although the line stretched some twenty cars long, each emitting distressed smoke signals of exhaust and signaling frustration through brake lights, not one of the delayed drivers honked or flashed their headlights, or even made an obscene gesture, as if everybody understood that Al's success at finding treasure served all of their best interests.

He sniffed the ground and blew aside crystals of snow. Where it had packed in, he melted the ice with the palm of his hand. Whenever Tank thought he saw something catch a sparkle, he pointed it out, and after a few minutes, Al had unearthed a quarter, two dimes, a nickel, and three pennies.

"That's enough for a cake donut," Tank said.

"Yeah, but..." Al shook the numbness out of his hands. "That's also almost half enough for a quart of malt liquor," he said, starting to transfer the money into his pocket.

"No sir." Tank grabbed his wrist. "You gotta do your duty, soldier."

"Okay, Sarge," Al said, and dumped the change onto the counter. "We're kicking some ass here today, ain't we?"

"That we most certainly are, sir."

Olentangy Al and Tank saluted each other, and Tank handed him the bag containing his paid-forward order, along with three breakfast sandwiches, which he paid for with his own money.

Al reached inside the bag, grabbed and unwrapped a sandwich, chomped down half of it in a single bite, then chewed with his mouth open, as if to better demonstrate his appreciation. Still chewing, he pulled the wagon off to the side, out of the way of the pickup window, but close enough so that he could watch. He stayed there until the next customer received the order he'd paid-forward.

"Mission accomplished," Al called out.

CHAPTER 7

11:30 AM

Ms. Johar had left three voicemail messages for her supervisor, each ending with an increasingly urgent request to "please call back," "please call back ASAP," and "I really need for you to call back immediately." Each time, she became more puzzled and disturbed by his failure to respond.

Mr. Jack Gentile served as the regional manager for Drip n' Donut franchises in Ohio, Indiana, and Michigan, exclusive of the hinterlands on the Upper Peninsula. Although she'd never met him, Ms. Johar felt she knew him from his weekly "Drip Notes" online newsletter, where he wrote about his inspiring personal visits to his stores, and observations of the good work being done by Drip 'n' Donuts employees throughout his region. She'd invited him repeatedly to visit the Cleveland Avenue shop—he'd already gone to Polaris three times, once even to Grove City—and he'd replied, via email, that he looked forward to doing so as soon as his schedule permitted. From time to time, whenever she had a suggestion for an improvement or wished to report a helpful hint or best practice, she posted to his blog, and he'd always responded with affirmative words like "Super!" and "That's the spirit!" Never before, though, had Ms. Johar felt compelled to contact him to resolve a problem—not that this was a problem, per se, more like a quandary.

Just what it was, *was*, in fact, what she wanted him to ask him.

All morning long, the office phone had been ringing off the hook, and every time Ms. Johar answered in her most professional voice, expecting the caller to be Jack Gentile. Almost all the calls had been from customers who wanted information about the pay-it-forward streak. Could they reserve a place in line? Could they use gift certificates? Could they pay-it-forward for delivery by Uber?

She'd grown as weary of the questions as she was of waiting for the call from Jack Gentile. Exasperated and wanting to escape from the ringing telephone, she pushed back her wheeled office chair, harder than she'd planned, for it rolled her right through the door.

Ms. Johar jumped up and brushed herself off, as if she'd meant to do that. Now, she felt committed to walking around.

It was somewhat gratifying, but also vaguely insulting, how Chavonne's shoulders tensed when Ms. Johar approached her from behind. Whatever Ximena and Huck were talking about, she noticed how they swallowed their words as soon as she drifted within earshot. As a matter of course, Tank kept his back turned to her as much as possible. Val just blushed like a naughty child caught awake after her bedtime.

Ms. Johar was well aware of the chilling effect her presence had upon her employees, but couldn't decide if they were acting childishly or conspiratorially. Either way, she didn't like it. Nor did she trust them.

She centered herself in front of the counter and, for something to do, rearranged the sugar packets in their dispenser. Then she wandered to the front windows and crossed her arms as she gazed out. Her heart fluttered when a Hummer limo entered the drive-thru, not the kind of vehicle she normally saw in this neighborhood. Maybe, she imagined, none other than Jack Gentile himself was a passenger inside.

Wouldn't that just be like him to drop whatever he'd been doing to make a personal appearance, incognito?

Even if she didn't really believe it, she decided to play it safe.

She went to Chavonne and said, "Please inform me when that limo has reached the front of the line. I would like to personally greet that particular customer."

"Why can't you cut the line?" Adam Erb griped to Jay-Rome when he saw the endless string of cars ahead of them.

"I don't think it works like that, boss."

"This will not abide." Adam clicked his tongue. "Look! Over there!" He pointed and said, "Call that security guard. I want to talk to him."

Jay-Rome powered down the window and hollered, "Yo, officer! Boss man here wants to talk with you."

The security guard had a road flag in one hand and a maple bar in the other. Instead of the standard issue brimmed hat that matched his Buzz Security, Inc. uniform, he wore a red stocking cap with a white ball on top. He shuffled his feet but didn't move forward.

Adam reinforced the request by sticking his arm out of the window and snapping his fingers. "Hurry up! Right now, please!"

The guard stuffed the rest of the maple bar into his mouth, hustled to the limo, and asked, "Is everything all right here, sir?"

"I need for you to direct traffic to make room for me at the front of the line. Time is of the essence. I'm in the middle of some urgent business, so I appreciate your prompt attention."

He handed the guard a crisp one hundred dollar bill.

Flabbergasted, the guard broke out into a grin so wide, it made his earlobes wiggle. "Is this for real? Are your bribing me?"

"Yes, but it is a limited time offer, so—"

"I've always wanted for somebody to bribe me!"

The guard gestured with his flag, beckoning Jay-Rome to follow while he led them. He held his flat palm forward and whistled, seeming pleased with himself. He led the limo past car after car, including: two dreadlocked women passing a joint in a Toyota Camry; a man wearing a "Muck Fichigan" baseball cap in jacked-up Jeep Wrangler Rubicon; a van from the Oak Gardens Convalescent Home; an Uber driver and his dozing passenger in a Mitsubishi; a couple of Somali men in a Fiat wearing their macawis over their coats; and several other vehicles. Drivers turned to look, to stare, to glower, or to shake their heads.

Adam waved at them as he passed. Nobody honked at the violation of protocol, although Adam Erb noticed and relished so many expressions of bafflement and mute perturbation.

"Pull straight up to the kiosk," he said to Jay-Rome. "I know exactly what I want to order."

11:35 AM

Huck cringed watching how Ms. Johar tangled herself in the headset cords while trying to put it on. She wore it backwards, and fumbled trying to adjust the microphone arm over her head.

Chavonne watched and giggled into her fist.

"Hello, hello, hello. Is this working?" Ms. Johar tried.

"Hello," replied a tentative voice in the earpiece.

Unable to bear it any longer, Huck helped Ms. Johar extricate herself from the cords and set the equipment right. Even with his assistance, though, she couldn't get the microphone to stay in place; it kept slipping under her neck. She wore the earpiece loosely, so that it leaked sound into the space outside her head.

"Good morning," she said into the microphone. "My name is Uma Johar, and I am the manager of this store. How can I make your morning great?"

Even through the tinny earpiece speaker, the voice on the other end oozed charm. It made Huck curious, a bit edgy.

"Good morning. Uma? From what I've heard through the grapevine, you've been making a lot of people's mornings great today, am I right?"

Ms. Johar seemed flattered. "Yes, that is true, but of course, that is our job — not just today, every day."

"Ab-suh-loot-lee! That's what I love about Drip 'n' Donuts. In fact, I love it so much that I'd like to take this opportunity to spread some Christmas joy, from me to all of Columbus."

"That is kind, sir, very noble of you. What would you desire to order?"

Huck could hear what sounded like a drum roll being slapped on the dashboard.

"I'd like to buy a dozen donuts for the next one hundred drive-thru customers, compliments of me, Adam Erb."

"*Adam Erb!*" Val squealed, and dropped a 24-ounce High Octane Berry Cooler onto her feet.

"Adam *fucking* Erb!" Huck shrieked, knocking a mocha cappuccino onto the ground.

"Who is Adam Erb?" Mrs Johar asked.

"Me. That's who," the suave voice answered. "Think of me as the donut Santa. I'm paying-it-forward."

"No way!" Huck cried. "I don't care who wears his lousy underwear. He can't buy us out. We can't let him do that."

"Why not?" Val asked.

"I agree with Huck," Ximena said, and Chavonne nodded her agreement.

Tank shook his head and mumbled, "No fuckin' way."

"There is no policy prohibiting him from purchasing every donut in the store, if that is his wish," Ms. Johar said.

From the speaker, Adam's voiced called, "Hello? Uma? Are you still there?"

Ms. Johar seemed flustered. "Yes sir. Thanks very much to you, sir—"

"Tell him to drive forward to the pickup window," Huck cut her off.

"Excuse me? Are you telling me what to do, Hyun-ki?"

"Let me deal with this, Ms. Johar."

She stepped toward him—to do what, Huck wondered—until the headset cord yanked her head backwards, and she turned around.

Huck hustled in front of the pickup window. The limo seemed as long as a train as the driver passed, then rows of tinted windows, finally reaching the last window, like a caboose, and stopped so that it was flush with the ledge. Huck looked down, face-to-face, with Adam Erb.

"You're not Uma Johar," Adam observed.

"No, my name is—"

Val squirmed by Huck, jostled for position front and center, and groped out the window to touch any part of Adam Erb she could reach.

"Hell-o, Mr. Erb," she sang. "I'm Val Vargas. So happy to meet you." She then whispered, "I'm wearing my Skivvies."

"Val. What a lovely name. I hope that you are satisfied."

"Oh, I am."

"And I really love your hair. What color is that?"

"Cotton candy."

"It looks good enough to eat."

Val tittered and waved a handful of her hair, as if inviting Adam to take a bite.

"Excuse me," Huck said.

Val didn't yield. "If you don't mind, Mr. Erb. Could I get a selfie with you?"

"It would be my distinct pleasure."

Val blushed, pushed Huck aside, and called for Ximena while waving her cell phone above her head. "Would you please, please, please snap a photo of me with Mr. Erb?"

"*Si Bueno*," Ximena said. "But will you also take one with me?"

Huck glared at her. "Not you, too?"

"Not for me," Ximena explained. "For my daughter, Tatiana. She wears those Skivvies."

"Me too," Chavonne interjected. "Who's this rich white boy, anyhow?"

Huck refused to join them in the photo, but Val, Ximena, and Chavonne took turns posing with him and snapping a volley of selfies. Adam Erb asked his driver to take one with everybody.

Ms. Johar paced behind them, *tsk*-ing, seeming impatient but reluctant to intervene.

"All right then," Huck said, shooing them away.

Adam handed a credit card to him.

Huck stood, hands in pockets, and stared him down. "I'm sorry, sir, but the policy of the pay-it-forward service limits orders to just individual customers at a time. That is, one person giving, one person receiving. We cannot accept advance sales. Also, all sales are anonymous. That is our policy."

"There must be some kind of a misunderstanding. May I speak to your manager?" Adam sat up and called, "Uma Johar?"

Ms. Johar pushed forward. "Yes sir."

"Would you please tell this young man to facilitate my request?"

Huck was shorter than Ms. Johar. He raised himself on his toes when she turned to face him.

Her eyes settled at the place where his nametag dangled. "Please do as Mr. Erb requests," she said with a slight quiver in her voice.

"I am sorry, Ms. Johar, but I cannot do that."

"What? Of course, you *can* do that, and as your supervisor, I am telling you that you *must*."

Ximena broke in. "But look, Ms. Johar, it says right there.... See?" She pointed to the rules posted next to the cash window.

Ms. Johar read them once, then again, the second time moving her lips.

Chavonne read for her, out loud. "Rule number one: Each customer must pay for at least one item on the menu for the next customer in line."

"Yes, I can read, but what are these rules? I am not aware of any such rules. I do not believe that we are within our legal rights to refuse service to any customer."

Huck said, "We are not refusing service—"

"Yes!" Adam clapped his hands. "That's that. Please charge my card. And after I leave, do not forget to tell every customer that their donuts were purchased just for them, compliments of Adam Erb."

Ms. Johar reached for Adam's credit card, but Huck snatched it before she could get it, shifted it to his other hand, and held it at arm's length.

"...But we *are* limiting it," he continued, "based upon reasonable principles of fairness."

Adam's smile disappeared. "This is some kind of joke, right?"

Meanwhile, Tank had left the kitchen and now stood behind Huck, glared down at Adam Erb, and in a combative voice said, "Listen, man, what about *can't* do it don't you understand?"

Ms. Johar backed away. She looked in turn to Ximena, to Chavonne, and to Val, but Ximena didn't blink, Chavonne folded her arms, and Val shrugged. Her authority seemed to vanish through her widening eyes.

Huck, on the other hand, felt like he'd been born for this moment.

"I am going to report this insubordination to the regional manager," Ms. Johar said, then scurried into her office.

"What the fuck?" Adam grumbled. "I've never heard of such nonsense." He puffed his chest. "Jay-Rome, let's get out of here."

"Wait," Huck called.

"So, have you come to your senses?"

"You have to pay-it-forward for the next order. Otherwise, you will break the chain. You wouldn't want to be responsible for doing that, would you?"

Adam looked behind him at the convoy of vehicles backed up across the mall, onto Cleveland Avenue, and ground his jaws together. "Okay, I'll buy a dozen donuts for just the next car, if that meets with your egg-headed socialist approval."

"*That*, I can do," Huck said.

CHAPTER 8

11:45 AM

Adam Erb felt as if his day had gotten off track. He had lots of important things to do—the negotiations with the National Football League were still in progress, he had an afternoon meeting scheduled with his R&D team at their skunk works lab in Gahanna, and he had committed to playing Santa Claus that evening at the Cow Town Milk Maids' annual Christmas benefit for the Girl Scouts of Ohio's Heartland. He was an A-list, in-demand catch for any engagement; his time extremely valuable. With a tweet, he could change people's whole lives, or at least he thought that he could— he'd never actually tested that supposition. Why, then, as he watched the Cleveland Avenue Drip 'n' Donuts store recede in the rear view mirror, did he feel jilted and insulted?

"Jay-Rome, turn around!" he snapped. "I want to go back."

"Say what, boss?"

"They must have misunderstood my proposal."

Adam could see Jay-Rome roll his eyes, even behind sunglasses.

"You sure that's somethin' you want to do, boss?"

"That's what I said."

"Boss, ain't rightly for me to say, but even so, I think you ought to leave this deal alone."

That was not what Adam wanted to hear. He sank into his seat and reached for the mini fridge, which he always kept stocked with orange juice, Red Bull, Bud Light, and an assortment of two-ounce liquor bottles. He grabbed and gulped a cinnamon whisky shot. It burned delightfully, all the way into his sinuses, opening new perspectives in his head.

"Fine! Then take me home."

"Home? What about...?"

"I'm canceling all of my meetings for the rest of the day, not that it is any of your business. Just drive, Jay-Rome."

"Okay," Jay-Rome said. "That's all I get paid to do."

11:50 AM

Under the present circumstances, closing the door to her office did not afford Ms. Johar the usual comfort. Normally, the closed door symbolized privilege and sanctuary, a place where her status permitted her to withdraw, answerable to nobody. She knew that when she closed her door, it looked bad to her employees, but that was the point—she didn't have to care what they thought. Faced with insubordination, though, it felt more like she'd holed up inside some dingy hideout, where the best she could hope for was to be ignored for the rest of the day. Mrs. Johar reasoned that confronting her employees about this pay-it-forward matter might make things worse. Better to ride out the crisis in hiding, then hope for better next time.

It wasn't her fault the situation had gotten out of control. If Jack Gentile had returned her calls and provided the necessary administrative support, she'd have been able to nip that whole seditious pay-it-forward boondoggle in the bud. This was yet another example of how she was disrespected and treated shabbily, just because her store happened to be in a less affluent part of town.

So, it was crystal clear to Ms. Johar that the company had abandoned her to fend for herself. Although she'd temporarily lost her authority over the staff, she still had one certain advantage—they all got off work at 2:00 PM. They would clock out, go home, and she'd stay on to direct the next shift, which, consisting of high school students and retirees, would be much more docile. All she had to do was wait them out. Time was on her side.

For the present, she busied herself with clerical tasks, like sorting mail, checking calendars, and drafting letters of reprimand that she would insert into each of her mutinous employees' personnel files. The only thing of consequence that she did was update and submit her orders for the afternoon delivery; that morning's unusually robust business had nearly depleted their inventory more rapidly than usual. Other than that, she planned to remain sequestered in her office and not come out for the rest of the shift. It was almost a relief that everybody was ignoring her.

11:55 AM
OH MY GOD!

Val spelled it out, because what had happened was too humongous for a mere OMG.

OH MY GOD! Just met #Adam_Erb @ D&D. Even more gorgeous in real life.

She attached the selfie that she'd taken with him, and then tweeted, texted, Instagram-ed, Facebook-ed, Pinterest-ed, and even changed her profile photos in honor of the occasion.

She was giddy. Adam Erb had called her "Val," not "Valerie" like it said on her name tag; it felt like they knew each other. Now, what mattered to she most in all the world was for him to *remember* her. Given his busy schedule and conflicting demands, Val worried he might forget her, so she convinced herself that, with a little perseverance and creativity, she could customize a memory just for him. First, she'd left a personal note written under the flap of his bag of donuts, for him to find when he opened it. Second, by flooding social media and attaching *#Feedthedeed* to every post, she hoped that the trend would attract his attention. It excited her to think that he might pluck her name from one of his online in-baskets and open a file containing the picture he'd taken with her, and maybe he'd pause to recall her smile, her hair, her sincerity, or even her boobs—whatever... she didn't care.

"Val," Huck called to her. "Pay attention. Your order is ready."

"Hold onto your horses," she said, but kept typing on her cell phone nonetheless.

Noon

Ximena knew that Tatiana hated it when she called during her lunch hour at school—it embarrassed her in front of her friends. According to Tatiana, it proved that she didn't trust her; it felt like she was checking up on her; it was a blatant invasion of her privacy... and just as soon as she turned 18 years old, she was going to be out of her mother's house, out of her life, out of her control, and there was not a fu... *freakin'* thing that Ximena could do about it. *Blah, blah, blah.*

Ximena ground her teeth while debating whether to call. It would practically guarantee yet another version of that same ongoing harangue. Maybe. However, this was not a call to scold her for something that she'd forgotten to do or to remind her of something that she had to do. This was different. The more Ximena thought about it, the more she convinced herself that Tatiana would resent her more for *not* calling under these circumstances. They'd both regret it if she didn't make that call.

She let the phone ring twelve times, hung up, counted to ten, then called again. This time, Tatiana answered on the first ring.

"*¡Ay!* What do you want, mother? I'm busy."

"I know, I know, I know. You are busy even when you are doing nothing."

"Oh. So you are calling me lazy? Did you call just to insult me? Couldn't you wait until tonight to dis' me?"

"*¡Mierda!* Listen to me, girl...." Ximena pulled the phone away from her mouth and took a cleansing breath before responding. "I called because there is an amazing thing happening here at where I work. People are doing things for each another. It is all over the internet. I want for you to come here after school, so that you can be a part of it."

"What is this about? Wait. Let me see."

Ximena envisioned Tatiana scrolling through screens on her phone.

"Mother, on my Facebook there is some story about people buying donuts to give away to strangers. One of my friends went through the line, and she posted that it is like a party."

"*Si*, just as I said. I want for you to see this, so you can one day later say that you were here. So, after school, *por favor*, do two things for me. First, call your Uncle Mateo and tell him to come here. I want for him to see this, too. Then, go to pick up Ignacio and Babette, and bring them here."

"Do you mean to say...?"

Ximena had been building up to this. "You have my permission to drive the car." She imagined Tatiana pumping her fist and mouthing *Yessssss*. "But do to be careful. It is starting to snow harder."

"Okay. Yes, I will, I will...." She hesitated before asking, "But mother, what if the party is over before I leave school?"

Looking out the window at the line of traffic that now extended to Innis Road in one direction and past the bowling alley in the other, Ximena assured her that, "This seems like it could go on and on forever."

12:10 PM

"Welcome to Drip 'n' Donuts. How can I make your afternoon great?"

Chavonne glanced in the fish-eye mirror and saw that the next vehicle at the kiosk was a shiny magenta Buick Le Sabre, modded with chrome-plated wheels, a shark's-tooth grille, and a ring of micro-blue LEDs around the license plate holder, where they illuminated the personalized plate, CRMNL. The car shook with booming bass notes.

"Do yah feel me?" she added.

"Oh yeah, I feel yah. Uh huh. You know it."

Even through the rap and throb of the music, the plush rhythm of the man's voice slipped into the center of her head and spread outward, as if he were kissing her with just his voice. She closed her eyes to hold onto that image.

"Hey, yo, like I said, I'm feeling yah, but are yah still hangin' with me here on planet Double D?"

Snapping herself out of it, Chavonne said, "Yeah, yo' yeah. I mean, what is it can I get for yo'?"

"Do yah really want me to answer that question?"

In the eighteen months that she'd worked at Drip 'n' Donuts, male customers in the drive-thru had hit on Chavonne countless times. At first, she'd been flattered. Over time, they started to annoy her. On that day, though, her whole attitude changed. She didn't think she ought to like it, but while her mind was sorting out her feelings, she heard herself answer, "Oh, yeah."

Naturally, the smooth operator in the Le Sabre ordered something sweet—chocolate frosted—and something gooey—honey-dipped sticky buns, not to mention half a dozen sugared "balls," by which he meant donut holes, although he sure seemed to like saying "balls." Lastly, he added an eggnog latte, extra sugar. When Chavonne told him to pull forward to the next window, he asked, "Will yah meet me there?"

Chavonne tossed aside her headset and, gesturing for Ximena to pick it up, explained that she had to hurry to the pickup window to meet a "friend." She pushed Huck out of the way, saying, "I got this order."

Ximena called, "You go, girl."

Huck looked at Chavonne, then at the Le Sabre that had just pulled to the pickup window, and he yielded his station to her.

Chavonne stood in window so that her breasts were at his eye level, the first things he saw when she slid it open.

The driver teased Chavonne, lowering the car's tinted windows a couple of inches, just enough to reveal the top of his head, then powered it back up. He repeated the game, showing a little more of himself each time, chuckling at Chavonne's agitation.

Finally, she said, "If yo' want your eggnog, yo' are goin' to have to lower that window enough so I can give it up."

The driver lowered the window all the way down. Snowflakes lighted and melted in his full afro. He sported a pencil-thin mustache over full lips, and a jeweled earring in his left earlobe. He brushed his hand against hers as he accepted the order. He was wearing diamond cufflinks.

"Ain't I seen you on the dance floor at the Electric Company before?" he asked.

"Me? No, I ain't never been. I like to dance, but not Leon."

"Leon?"

Chavonne wanted to slap herself. So far, she'd kept the whole transaction on the up and up, but when she'd named Leon by name, she knew that she ought to feel a little guilty for flirting. At the same time, she worried that by mentioning Leon, she would discourage the driver. She tilted her head and shrugged one shoulder.

"Well, you don't need Leon to go to the Electric Company. If you want to dance, just get up and go. When you do, ask anybody for Eldridge." He brushed his mustache with his pinky finger. "That's me."

"Maybe."

"Hope so." Eldridge doubled the pay-it-forward order for the next person in line.

12:15 PM

While waiting for Tank to finish an order for Belgian waffles, Huck leaned against the cooler, took his cell phone out of his pocket, and googled "pay-it-forward drive-thru records." He read an article about a Starbucks in St. Petersburg, Florida, where 783 customers paid forward in a streak that lasted over fourteen hours. He sighed and shook his head.

"Do you think we can break the record, kid?" Tank asked.

Startled, Huck cleared the screen.

"Not *that* record, but that's not fair, either. Starbucks? Big deal. That's just coffee. We compare more closely to a fast food restaurant. In that category, so far as I can tell, the record is 513, set at a Chick-Fil-A in Georgia. We're already a third of the way there. We could do it."

"I don't blame you for thinking big, kid, but come on...." Tank tsk-ed, a little puff of air inflating his face mask. "Do you mind?" he asked, removing the mask's elastic bands from behind his ears. "I can't stand wearing this goddamned face thingy."

Huck shrugged. "What do you mean, *come on*? You don't think we can do it?"

"Look, kid, it's great what we've got going here today, all this peace on Earth and joy to the world happy horse shit. I'm down with it. But take it from an old foot soldier... if the top brass ain't got your back, you're going to fail."

"Yeah, Ms. Johar...."

"I ain't talking about her. I'm talking about *you*."

It made Huck twitch to think of himself as belonging to any category of rank that included "top brass."

Tank continued. "You got to have a very clear plan and an end game. Do you want to break that record? Sure, it'd be quite an accomplishment. It'd give us all ten minutes of fame. But how do you expect to do it? And what happens if you do?"

Huck recoiled from these questions, because he'd asked himself the exact same things. Tank was the last person whom he expected to challenge him intellectually, and not only was he thinking the same things, but he was demanding answers.

Tank continued. "And do you have a backup plan? Because right now, I double dog guarantee you that somewhere out there in this hick metropolis, there's some twisted son of a bitch with a Grinch's heart who is thinking to himself right now that it'd be a great idea to kill this hippie dippy paying-the-kumbaya-love-forward-drive-thru thing, and he may be the next person who pulls up to the window. That's true and you know it."

Tank's comments rang true, and it made Huck wonder just how in the hell this country kept losing wars when they were being fought on the front lines by guys as perceptive as Tank. It must take a really fucked-up top brass to do that.

"Am I right?" Tank asked, wrapping a Belgian Waffle sandwich.

Huck snapped his fingers and said, "I need to contact the press."

CHAPTER 9

12:30 PM

Ernest Erb shook his hips and clenched his buttocks, while rocking his wheelchair back and forth in an arduous but futile effort to induce a fart. In that moment, the pent up gas gurgling in his bowels mattered more to him than his mind-numbing boredom, or that he could feel bugs crawling across his scalp, or that the Velcro band on his Drawers was tugging on his pubic hairs, or that he wanted to put his fist through the goddamned television—that's how sick he was of *The Price is Right*. His gastrointestinal distress had grown so profound that it even displaced the nearly constant mental rants and tirades against his son that dominated his thoughts all day long, every day. He spent most of his days like that, with problems backing up as if waiting their turns to torment him.

Expelling the gas bubble clotted in his guts felt like a matter of life and death. He knew from experience that clots could kill. A blood clot in his brain had already almost done him in once. The embolism struck him down right in the middle of blowing his nose. Two weeks later, when he awakened from a coma to learn that he'd suffered a stroke, his first stupid thought was that he'd been jerking off too hard. A stroke? That sounded to him like wanking. Only later did he realize that, no... in fact, it meant that he'd never be able to jerk off again, among other things. Oh, what he wouldn't give for just one last fat, throbbing erection and a functional right hand to make it worthwhile.

If he could only fart and cum at the same time, that would be heaven.

Inspired by that desire, Ernest re-directed his clenching, rocking, and grunting from the rear to the front, in the hopes of encouraging wood. What else did he have left to do all day long, but fart, watch *The Price is Right*, and dream about getting a boner?

"Here, Dad, I brought you some donuts," his son said, putting a tray onto his lap and fastening it to the side of his wheelchair. "I know I'm not supposed to, but I figured what the hell, one can't hurt. I got your favorite, lemon custard-filled."

Ernest pawed and poked at the donut, managing to insert the bent middle finger on his somewhat good hand into the donut's asshole — that's what he called the orifice where the baker inserted the filling — and pulling out a glob of custard. He hoped his son realized that he was doing this on purpose, that it wasn't just lack of motor control causing him to fling the yellowish slop off his middle finger. If his son interpreted the act to be flipping him the bird, he wouldn't be wrong.

Unfortunately, his son seemed incapable of understanding an insult. Ernest belched "Fah fah fah oog uhk oog uhk wooooooo" — that is, "fuck you," but his son never seemed to have a clue.

He was an ignorant little fucker, if he even *was* his son... which Ernest doubted, because his ex-wife, Adam's mother, was a filthy whore. She might have been screwing any number of men at the time, before she got lucky and finally screwed one who just happened to be a multi-millionaire. Ernest figured that had been her plan all along, to hump and debauch her way out of their working-class neighborhood and into a suburban mansion.

Fuck it! I'm better off without her.

What really stung, though, was how at the time of the divorce, Adam, who was just nine years old, chose to go live with his mother, like a traitorous little prick, not a son of his.

And what was the deal with his son always bringing him donuts, anyway? Did he think he was being clever, because everybody knew that cops liked to hang out at donut shops? Wrong. Back when he'd walked the beat in North Columbus, Ernest avoided the donut shops, because he thought it gave the good cops like him a lazy reputation. Instead, Ernest took his breaks at Stan's "Good Food" Diner on Route 3, where as soon as he walked in, Flo, the waitress, served up his "usual," a piece of Dutch apple pie with vanilla ice cream on top—he didn't even having to ask for it. What he wouldn't give for a slice of apple pie, right then and there, instead of that mushy donut. But did his so-called son ever bring him a piece of apple pie? No. Greedy little backstabbing cocksucker that he was.

"Sit still, Dad. You're going to fall out of your chair again."

He should be so lucky as to fall out of his chair. It would be the most exciting thing to happen to him in years. What did the little fucker think would happen if he fell, anyway? He wouldn't break. He was still a cop, and proud to wear a badge, even if it was just a chintzy tin star pinned to his pajamas top. It still stood for something to him. Besides, all that he wanted in life—

other than to fart, and to get an erection, and a slice of apple pie — was to get the hell out of that chair. Falling down would be better than sitting there like dead weight all day, every day. Crawling would be better. If he could raise himself onto his own two feet just once more in his life, Ernest would kick his son as hard as he could right in the ass.

As Ernest shook and shifted in the wheelchair, the knots in his intestines tightened and gastric bubbles churned, until at once, he felt awash with a semi-fluid release.

Ernest Erb had messed himself.

"Dad! For cryin' out loud!"

"Fah fah fah oog uhk oog uhk wooooooo."

CHAPTER 10

1:05 PM

Jack Gentile owed a debt to Adam Erb for what either turned out to be the best or the worst thing that ever happened to him, depending on his ever-changing point of view. Adam had introduced Jack to his first wife, Lorraine—an ex-girlfriend of his, but Jack didn't mind taking Adam's discards. Each of them was an upgrade over the women who usually dated him. When Adam left them for any of a myriad of reasons, Jack was there to console them. The method worked so well for Jack that he felt obligated to ask Adam to be best man at his wedding.

Once, Jack had loved Lorraine with all his heart and believed that she was his soulmate. She gave him everything he wanted. For the first three years of their marriage, she worked as a waitress at Denny's, supporting him while he was in business school. After he graduated and got his first job, she bore him two perfect children and kept a pristine household. However, after ten years of marriage, just when he was getting established as an up-and-coming young executive in the Drip 'n' Donuts business empire, she accelerated her spending to match his increasing salary. Among those expenses was a significant investment in therapy, which ultimately led her to conclude that he was responsible for ruining her life. She thus seemed to take special venom in suing him for divorce, custody, and back-breaking alimony.

From the emotional wreckage, though, Jack found new romance with a younger and more worshipful woman, whom he loved with all his heart and believed to be his soulmate, and who had the additional virtue of having no prior connection whatsoever to Adam Erb. Still, Jack wasn't sure if he had fully repaid that original debt to Adam, or if time and circumstances had nullified it. All in all, it was complicated. The only simple thing in the whole briar patch of thorny relationships was that when Adam called wanting a favor, Jack felt obliged to answer.

"Hello, A-man. How's the view from Erb-ia?" was Jack's standard greeting for Adam.

"It's all peaches and cream," was Adam's standard reply.

Jack gazed out of his office window in One Seagate in Toledo at the picturesque Maumee River, where nobody was fishing. If he wasn't working, that's what he'd be doing.

"Are you aware of what is going on at one of your stores in Columbus?"

Jack had no idea what he was talking about. "Of course, I do. I'm the regional manager... but tell me what you've heard."

"I'm talking about that pay-it-forward streak."

How did he not know about this? Jack opened his email and scanned subject lines for a clue. There were, in fact, several messages with the subject "Pay-it-Forward."

"Polaris?" he wondered aloud.

"That's what you'd expect, right? I mean, that's the newest, fanciest, and most hip donut shop in the whole metro area. But, no, it's down in Linden, in that old 1960s strip mall on the north side. Apparently, it has been going on since early this morning. The story is all over the internet."

"No shit. Linden, for cryin' out loud. I've never been there. Is it really as scuzzy as I've heard?"

"Unfortunately, yes. I know that area pretty well. Oh, it isn't all bad, apart from the refugees, rednecks, street gangs, white trash, homeless people, and welfare cheats, that is."

"Be careful, Adam. Those are my customers you're talking about. Statistically, lower income populations consume more donuts per capita."

"No offense intended. But, Jack, I went down there myself—you know I like to keep it real, right?—and I was shocked that when I tried to pay-it-forward in my own way, some skinny Asian kid who looked like he was fourteen years old *refused* to take my money."

"Huh? We take *everybody's* money. What happened?"

"I just wanted to make a charitable contribution to the cause, that's all. You know, peace on Earth and happy holidays, right? So, I offered to buy a dozen donuts for the next one hundred customers in the drive-thru. Pretty generous, if I do say so myself, but that kid told me that I couldn't do it. He mentioned some policy that I think he made up, something about paying-it-forward being anonymous and restricted to one-to-one transactions. Some shit like that."

The whole time that Adam had been talking, Jack was catching up on the string of emails from Uma Johar, who, as memory served, was the manager of that store in Linden. Essentially, the theme of her correspondence was that she wanted to be told what to do.

"Listen, Jack, I'm just telling you this because I know that, as a businessman who takes his company's image very seriously, you would want to know if you've got a problem. Well, this is a problem. The inmates are running the asylum."

"I see." He opened an email from Uma Johar with the subject line EMERGENCY!!! "Tell you what I'm going to do, Adam. I'll call the manager of that store and set things right. I'm not sure how I feel about this pay-it-forward business. Done right, it would be great publicity. But it could also get out of hand."

"That's my point. Good talking to you, Jack. Give my best to Lorraine."

"Lorraine and I are divorced. Remember? I'm now married to Heather."

"Right. That's what I meant to say, no matter what I said."

1:15 PM

"Asshole," Adam Erb muttered to himself after hanging up with Jack Gentile. He pushed back his desk and started tapping his foot while thinking.

What should I do next?

On one hand, he could just let the matter drop. There was still time for him to play Santa Claus for the Milk Maids, whom he really hated to disappoint. On the other hand, he was still pissed by how rudely they'd treated him at the Drip n' Donuts in Linden, when all that he'd wanted to do was to buy a dozen donuts for a lousy one hundred people. What they'd done was wrong. Worse than being just wrong, though, was that it had been done to *him*. Letting the matter drop wasn't in his repertoire.

"Jay-Rome!" he called.

There was no response, so Adam went looking for him. There were only a few rooms in the house where Jay-Rome was permitted to go—the kitchen, the downstairs bathroom, the sun room, and, finally, his father's room, which was where he found him, sitting across a table from the old man, playing cards.

"What are you doing?"

"Just playing five card stud with your father. He's real good at bluffin'. Kind of like the Rain Man."

"That isn't bluffing. That vacant look is his normal state. He doesn't know what he's doing."

"Not so, boss. He's done beat me six hands in a row."

Adam looked quizzically at his father, who put his middle finger into his mouth and made disgusting sucking noises.

"I think you're reading too much into his burps and grunts."

"Nuh-uh, boss. I can understand him. You gotta imagine like he's speaking with his mouth full."

"I don't believe you."

Ernest Erb said, "Fah fah fah oog uhk wooooo."

"What did he just say?"

Jay-Rome winked at Ernest, then turned to Adam and said, "He said thank you."

Adam rather hoped it was true, because gratitude implied forgiveness, and that was what he really wanted from his father.

"Never mind, Jay-Rome. Get the limo. I need for you to drive me somewhere."

"Where we goin' this time, boss?"

"Back to the Drip 'n' Donuts—the one at Polaris, that is."

"Again? You sure got donuts on the head today, boss."

"Keep your wiseass remarks to yourself."

Adam sat across the card table from his father, placed his hand on the old man's shoulder, looked him in the eye and said, "You're very welcome, Dad."

1:30 PM

Ms. Johar had plugged her headphones in, and was listening to *Tunak Tunak Tak* when she noticed the light flickering on her office phone, indicating an incoming call. That afternoon, she'd already ignored so many calls without the slightest regard that she just closed her eyes and let the song sweep her back to sunny Delhi. A couple of seconds later, she snapped out of her reverie when she suddenly realized that the name on the caller ID was *Jack Gentile*.

She jumped out from under her headphones and lunged to answer the phone before it skipped into voicemail.

"Hello," she gasped.

"Uma Johar? This is Jack Gentile, your regional manager. I'm so pleased to finally make your acquaintance."

"Indeed, it is my honor." Aware that her voice was breaking, she cleared her throat. "Ahem. I know that a person in your position is extremely busy, so I thank you for making time for me. I do have a certain situation here today that has given me concern."

"Yes, I've heard. So, it sounds like Christmas has come early at your store. Is this pay-it-forward phenomenon still ongoing?"

Ms. Johar looked out the window and surmised by the length of the line at the drive-thru that it was.

"Yes, it seems to have become—how do you say—*viral*. I must say that I have been conflicted about it. Sales are excellent. However, there have been some complications."

"Yes. For example, is it true that you had a customer who your staff refused to accept forward payment for a large number of orders?"

Ms. Johar couldn't tell from his voice if that was a sincere question or an implied criticism. She wanted to assert that none of this was her fault. She wished that she had the nerve to tell Mr. Gentile that if he'd answered her first call, then none of those troubling complications would ever have occurred. Or, she could always blame Huck.

"It was not as simple as that—"

"Uma. May I call you Uma? And, please, call me Jack. Anyway, Uma, don't get me wrong. I am all in favor of sharing goodwill and donuts. Also, I can't complain about the free publicity. I do worry, though, about the precedent that you're setting. To my knowledge, this has never happened at any Drip 'n' Donuts franchise, anywhere. We need to take care not to let good intentions cause us to compromise good business practices. I worry that the longer this pay-it-forward streak lasts, the harder it will be to manage. I don't want it to become a circus."

Although she agreed with everything he said, she didn't see how she could say so without incriminating herself. She felt trapped in a classic lose-lose situation. "What do you suggest for me to do?"

"It would probably be best if you were to find some gentle, non-confrontational way to end it. That shouldn't be too hard. All it takes is one person to break the streak, right?"

He made it sound so simple. Ms. Johar knew for sure that if she left her office and issued an edict to her staff to accept no more forward payments, they would argue and refuse. She checked the clock—there was just half an hour to go before the start of the next shift. That was her best chance and her easiest way out.

"It will be done, sir," Ms. Johar assured him. "And please, I'd like to invite you to visit our shop, at your soonest convenience. There are many things I'd like to discuss with you."

"Of course," he said, which was neither yes nor no.

1:40 PM

Nothing was happening at the drive-thru at the Polaris Drip 'n' Donuts , which, Adam supposed, was more or less normal for the middle of the day in the middle of the week during the darkest month of the year. Still, it disappointed him since it had already been fifteen minutes since he'd tweeted:

> *Att'n Erbs! Early Xmas goodies fr moi @*
> *Polaris D'n'D, 2:00 pm 2day.*
> *#spread_the_joy.*

By his reckoning, fifteen minutes should have been enough time for his followers to have mobilized. Sometimes he loved them; sometimes he pitied them; sometimes he felt responsible for them; but no matter how he felt about them at any given time, he'd come to depend upon them to do his bidding. Adam wondered if perhaps they were confused between his latest tweet and his earlier one, also on the subject of donuts. To clarify, he followed up with a second:

All Erbs! Meet moi @ Polaris D'n'D. NOW! #spread_the_joy.

That ought to get their hormones and endorphins flowing, he thought.

"Jay-Rome, please park the car," he commanded. "Not there. Closer. Over there."

"Boss, that space is for handicapped."

"Do you see any handicapped here? No? Then unless you plan to alert the state highway patrol of my malfeasance, do as you're told and park."

"Jeez, okay, boss. Ain't no fuzz off my back."

Adam buttoned his coat, wrapped a scarf around his face, and put on a red Santa hat.

"Wait here," he said. "I may be a while."

Apparently, the staff of the Polaris Drip 'n' Donuts had not heard that he was coming , for when he entered, expecting cheers and fanfare, he received only a weary look from a forlorn, fiftyish cashier with a teardrop tattoo under her left eye. Adam didn't recognize her from that morning.

"Welcome to Drip 'n' Donuts," she intoned. "How can I make your afternoon great?"

At that instant, however, Phoebe, the girl who'd served Adam earlier that morning, caught sight of him and skipped over to the counter.

"Adam Erb twice in the same day! It's, for sure, a real miracle!"

That got everybody's attention. Led by Phoebe and Pandora, the rest of the staff converged at the front counter. They stood facing Adam like a police lineup.

"Welcome back to Drip 'n' Donuts, Mister Erb," Ms. Doody said. "To what do we owe this second visit today?"

Adam strutted to the corner of the counter where Phoebe and Pandora were giggling and making bug eyes at each other. He worked his way between them and draped an arm over each, announcing, "I am here to pay-it-forward. I will buy one dozen donuts, free to each of the next one hundred customers. It's all on me. Merry Christmas from Adam Erb."

Adam lifted his chin and turned so that his best side was facing forward. Phoebe and Pandora hugged him from the left and the right, exalting "amazeballs," "awesome sauce," and "totally bedazzling." They mauled him with hugs and pinches.

Ms. Doody stepped back to examine the racks of donuts on display behind the counter, counting with her fingers to take quick inventory.

"Yes sir, Mr. Erb," she said. "We can do that. I'll just have to supplement the afternoon delivery. Fortunately, there is still time for me to call it in."

"If you have any problem, just let me know and I'll contact my buddy, Jack Gentile, and I'm sure that he can fix things."

"That's good to know."

"Oh, look," Adam said. "There's a customer at the window now. May I do the honors?"

With Phoebe and Pandora bouncing up and down next to him like elves, Adam tossed the ball on his Santa hat over his shoulder so that it hung in front of his chest.

"Welcome to Drip 'n' Donuts," he said to the nonplussed customer in the drive-thru. "I'm Adam Erb, and I'm going to make your afternoon great."

1:45 PM

Huck had already decided that he would not leave when his shift ended at 2:00 PM. He'd invested too much heart and soul in the pay-it-forward streak to clock out and walk away, as if he could just hand over something so fragile and precious to the care of the next crew. The streak was something worthy of his ideals and aspirations — he needed it, and it needed him.

Ms. Johar, though, would probably forbid it, even if he waived his right to receive overtime wages — hell, even if he offered to work for free. To continue, he would have to make a stand, and if he had to sit right on top of the counter and refuse to budge, in the spirit of so many of his non-violently resisting heroes from the past, that's what he'd do. He almost hoped it would come to that, for the glory that came with standing up for a cause.

He recalled the words of Emma Goldman: "Idealists are foolish enough to throw caution to the wind, and by doing so have advanced mankind and enriched the world." He was eager to be that kind of a fool.

So, when Ms. Johar emerged from her office at a quarter to the hour and started erasing the names of the first shift and writing assignments for the second onto the master schedule, Huck emboldened himself with a slug of XXX high octane dark java and marched over to confront her.

"Please, no," Huck said, taking her hand to stop her from expunging his name on the board. "I.m staying."

Tank, the next nearest to them, put down his spatula to listen.

"There is no need for that, although thank you, Hyun-ki. We shall be adequately staffed."

"I know, but... I can't quit while people are still paying-it-forward. *I won't.*"

Ms. Johar stiffened and dug in her heels. "I cannot allow that. You must realize that there is nothing more for you to do. Soon this business will be over, and then it will be as if it never happened."

Huck so seldom raised his voice that he felt a palpable rush of adrenaline when he amplified, "Nothing happened? So far, two hundred and eighty citizens have joined this movement! Each and every one of them is invested in keeping it alive. They all share a piece of the dream! Through their words and actions, for no other reason than a desire to share their love with fellow human beings, they have created something to unite all of Columbus. Together, we are strong! We are glad! We are proud! I am not leaving!"

Tank started clapping slowly, saying, "That was beautiful, kid."

Then Ximena joined in clapping, followed by Chavonne, and a woman waiting at the pickup window whose dog also barked, and then, finally, by Val.

"I'm staying, too," Tank said, "at least until Happy Hour starts at the Zig Zag Club."

"And I will stay," Ximena said. "My daughter is coming after school, and I want to be here when she arrives."

"I will not stand for this!" Mrs Johar insisted. "You all must leave, or I shall fire you all!"

Tank said, "It wouldn't be the first time that I refused to obey a direct order."

Ms. Johar wrung her hands, then tried another tact. "But what about the next shift? They expect to work, to earn their wages. What would you tell them?"

Huck had already anticipated this problem.

"We can pay them the equivalent of their regular wages with the cash in our escrow fund. We have enough to do that."

Chavonne jumped in. "I done said that money is for tips."

"Really, Chavonne? We have to do the right thing. We've accomplished nothing if we do less." Huck swallowed, tempering his voice. "Besides, we've exceeded our regular tips by four times the normal amount. It's as if the people are thanking us for what we're doing. We can't be greedy. People trust us."

"Perhaps you were not listening!" Ms. Johar interjected. "It is up to me alone to determine how to allocate those funds."

"Why don't you join us?" Huck said to her, offering his hand.

"But of course not!"

Ms. Johar slapped Huck's hand away, but he held it level.

Ximena put her hand on top of Huck's.

Tank cracked his knuckles, said, "Happy hour don't start until 5:00, anyhow," and added his hand to the pact.

Chavonne huffed and vouched that, "I am just only stayin' for them 'xtra tips," before wiping her hand with her apron and joining the covenant.

Val, meanwhile, was scrolling through screens on her cell phone. "You guys are, like, really serious about this thing, huh?" She looked as if, despite all evidence to the contrary, she still worried that they were playing an elaborate prank on her.

"You're a part of this, too," Huck assured her.

"Oh, well, okay. I mean, I did get to meet Adam Erb, so that was special," Val said, placing her hand on the top of the stack.

Ms. Johar stood with her arms crossed and her jaw clenched. She opened her eyes wide, staring all five of them down at once. The stalemate lasted just a couple of seconds. When Huck looked away from her, so did the others.

"Okay, team," Huck said. "One! Two! Three!"

"Feed the Deed!" they all exclaimed in unison, waving their hands above their heads like the wings of soaring birds.

Ms. Johar fled into her office and slammed the door behind her.

1:58 PM

Such effrontery! Such impudence! Such brazen and shameless contempt for authority!

Ms. Johar felt her indignation rise until it burst. "Children of dogs!" she shouted at the backside of the door. "Worms and lizards! Feeders on road kill!"

It's intolerable! It's unfathomable! It's incorrigible, unscrupulous, and outrageous!

She wrung her hands and kicked over a garbage can, screaming, "Scabrous monkeys! Diseased jackals!"

She considered calling back Jack Gentile to give him a piece of her mind. If he had done his job by answering her earlier calls, this mutiny would never have happened. It was his fault as much as anybody's. "Sucker on the teats of cows," she muttered, enjoying that image.

The more that she cursed, though, the more clearly she realized the futility of her situation. Divested of her status, exposed for a weakling, she felt like she might as well be invisible. How had her fortunes turned so dramatically in just a few hours? Every payment forward had chipped away a little more at her moral authority, breaking the caste order of her world. The events of the day revealed her to be worse than an untouchable—an inconsequential.

She still had the power to to execute one final act of reprisal, though—her parting shot, as it were. She logged onto the Drip 'n' Donuts administrative users' web page and cancelled the afternoon delivery.

Finished, she put on her coat and scarf and escaped out the back door, leaving without goodbyes. It was a relief knowing that whatever happened next, she would not have to deal with it.

CHAPTER 11

2:10 PM

The longer it lasted, the weirder it got. The drive-thru streak inspired playfulness, parody, and a certain dramatic silliness that compelled folks to vie for new and original ways to order donuts. Many went scrambling back into their closets for their Halloween costumes. Among the various characters from history, mythology, and popular culture to visit the drive-thru to pay-it-forward were: Homer Simpson and Guy Fawkes; Mahatma Gandhi and Johnny Appleseed; the Pope and Barack Obama; a drag queen, Wonder Woman, Darth Vader, Bette Boop, Kermit the Frog, Lady Liberty, and Elvis, skinny and fat.

A scrawny, curly-haired minstrel with a cigarette behind his ear and wearing a harmonica holder around his neck sang his order in a gritty twang:

> *I'm getting hungry, too hungry to see*
> *Feel like I'm knocking on Donuts door*
> *Knock, knock, knocking on Donuts door*

And an eerie, mulatto King of Pop wearing a surgical mask, a red leather jacket, and a white sequined glove got out of his car and spun on his heels, attempting to moonwalk, while singing:

> *Thriller! Filler Up!*
> *Ain't no one gonna stop me*
> *From stuffin' donuts up my butt*

There were even a couple of Adam Erb imposters wearing only their Drawers under their coats. Still, for all the personas and pretenders, those that Huck had seen go by most often were S. Claus and J. Christ. Santa tended to appear behind the wheel of minivans or sports utility vehicles, and Jesus in coupes or sedans. By Huck's unofficial tally, so far he'd seen a dozen Santas and nine Jesuses, the latter in both infant and adult versions.

But he'd never expected to see Santa and Jesus arrive together, sitting side-by-side in the front of a Geo Metro, their elbows sharing the narrow armrest between their seats.

"Ho, ho, ho," Santa said.

"Peace be with you," Jesus said.

"What can I get for you gentlemen?" Huck asked.

"Joy to the world!" they both proclaimed.

"Right on," Huck said. "But pastry-wise, what can I get for you?"

Santa leaned across the seat to consult with Jesus.

Huck noticed that Santa was, in fact, a woman wearing a kitschy fake beard, although she did have the requisite red cheeks and bulbous nose. Jesus had a real beard, although it was patchy and he was balding on top. If either of them could have been characterized as having a belly like a bowlful of jelly, it was the Jesus impersonator. Santa was actually kind of bony. They discussed in whispers, as if comparing notes on their naughty/nice lists, before nodding when they reached an agreement.

"We don't want anything for ourselves," Santa said. "We're just here to pay-it-forward."

"The only gift worth giving is one given to a stranger," Jesus added.

Huck made a mental note to write that down. "Okay," he said, "but part of the grace in paying-if-forward is accepting what others have given. The last customer paid ahead two pecan sticky buns, just for you."

Santa and Jesus high-fived each other.

"It's nice to know that somebody actually still believes in us," Jesus said.

"Amen," Huck testified.

2:20 PM

Edgar brought the whole damn band. The Scioto River Bottom Dwellers Jug Band was a folk and old time string band that played Americana, depression-era talking blues, labor union songs, 60s protest music, and square dance tunes at politically correct bars, markets, coffee shops, arts galleries, street fairs, and special events all around Columbus, usually for tips and/or contributions to Greenpeace, Planned Parenthood, the Southern Poverty Law Center, and/or the Democratic Socialists of America. The band wasn't very good, but that hardly mattered, for listening to them was an act of faith. The core of the ensemble consisted of Edgar on the fiddle and his sister, Eileen, playing the five-string Scruggs-style banjo. Other musicians came and went, a different ensemble for every occasion. Even Huck, who was tone deaf and musically illiterate, occasionally joined them, rattling a beat on the washboard. Every Bottom Dwellers gig was party. Even those listeners who had no sympathy for their politics easily got swept up in their feisty spirit, and with halfhearted effort, anybody could get laid after the show. That's how it had started for Edgar and Huck.

When Huck saw Edgar's van park in front of the shop and the band started unloading their instruments, he thought *uh oh*. That wasn't quite what he'd expected when he told Edgar to "spread the word." He asked Ximena if she could cover the pickup window, while he hurried to meet Edgar as he was coming through the door.

"Felicitations, Huckster!" Edgar shouted, leaning forward to give Huck an affectionate peck.

Huck accepted the kiss with tightly closed lips. "Thanks for coming, but this isn't what I expected."

Whenever Edgar grinned, it looked like his lower jaw came unhinged and his teeth grew to fill the gaps.

"We're just getting started," he declared. "This is going to be huge, Huckster. Definitely potentially more huge than Occupy, or the Million Persons' March, or Democracy Springtime...." He started to pant. "Okay, then, where can we set up?"

"Set up?"

"Yeah. At first, we thought that we'd play outside on the patio, but it's too damn cold out there. How about if we shift those two tables together and move around a couple of chairs to give ourselves some room?"

Bottom Dwellers instantly started lifting and moving furniture in compliance with Edgar's instructions.

"But, listen Huckster, don't let us get in the way. What you're doing here is way too important. We're just here to help out. Feed the Deed!"

Huck backed away, bumping into Tank after just a couple of steps.

"What's all of this bullshit?" Tank asked.

Huck recognized the "what the fuck" look on Tank's face—part disgust, part amusement, part judgment, and part dumbfoundment. His jaw dropped like he'd vomited something bigger than his head.

"This is the band," Huck said.

Amid a piercing cacophony, the Bottom Dwellers began tuning their instruments.

"Yeah." Tank ran his eyes over the band members—over Eileen, twice. "Listen, kid, you know that I'm normally the last person to give a rat's ass about protocol. Still, I'm just saying that you really ought to at least mention what's going on to old lady Johar before she comes out of her office with a flame thrower."

"Maybe you're right," Huck conceded. "I don't suppose that you'd like to—"

"Not me, kid. This is your mess."

Ms. Johar's door might as well have been sealed with a curse, so few people ever entered her office when it was closed. She had a way of shutting the door with purpose, never leaving even the slightest crack ajar, so that it was effectively a wall. This, the staff assumed, she did to signal that she was not to be interrupted. What it really meant to them, though, was that she didn't give a damn about what they did or what was going on in the shop, so long as they left her alone. In that respect, her closed door represented a kind of freedom, for if she could ignore them, then they could return the favor.

Huck made a tight fist and knocked on Ms. Johar's door. He stepped back while waiting, then waited some more, counting to ten before he knocked again, this time harder and longer. Glancing over his shoulder, he saw that the rest of the crew was watching and waiting, too.

"Just go in," Tank said.

Cracking the door, Huck called "Hello?"

Receiving no response, he opened it a bit wider.

"Ms. Johar?"

Finally, he pushed it open all the way, went in, walked all around the desk, looked under it, looked behind her filing cabinet, and even pushed aside the garments hanging on the coat rack looking for her. Stymied, Huck steadied himself against a bookshelf and faced the others, who had all gathered in the threshold.

"She's gone," he announced.

Chavonne said, "That ol' bitch done snuck out the back door, running away like chicken shit."

Val added, "I can't believe that she'd do that."

Ximena said, "I can believe it. She had that look on her face, like she knew that she was *terminado*."

Tank took in a long breath through the nose, as if it helped him think. Sitting at Ms. Johar's desk, he put up his feet, pointed at Huck, and said, "Now this is your show, kid."

"Me?" Huck caught a glimpse of his reflection in Ms. Johar's framed diploma from the Indian Institute of Management, which was hanging at eye level on the wall behind her desk. He thought: *This is my show? Does that make me* the man?

The man was something he'd never wanted to be.

The phone rang on Ms. Johar's desk. Again. Again.

"Are you gonna answer that?" Tank asked.

Huck lifted the phone's receiver with both hands. By answering this call, Huck felt as if he was opening himself up for some sinister capitalist virus to enter his body. How should he answer? Generally, he'd always kind of liked the "How can I make your day great" greeting—amiable and positive, it encouraged a kind of affirmative mutualism. Still, it was also canned and corporate, no doubt the product of some unscrupulous publicist and tested with an unwitting focus group. So now, Huck realized, was his chance to improve upon it. He held the phone against his chin, thinking.

"Greetings, comrade," he finally said. "I'm Huck. How can I be of service?"

The caller did most of the talking. Huck bounced his head while listening. He grunted "oh," mumbled "hmmm," stammered "uh huh," and then concluded, "Okay, then. Yeah, see you soon."

He hung up the phone and announced to the others:,"Hey, everybody, we're going to be on television!"

3:05 PM

The bright blue, extra-long cargo van bearing the "Eyewitness News" gigantic eyeball logo on its side U-turned on Cleveland Avenue, cut across the center line as it swung into the strip mall, then forced its way through the pay-it-forward queue, finally screeching to rest in the middle of two parking spaces in front of the store.

"They're here," Huck called.

"Oh my good gracious, this is really happening," Val sputtered, while touching up her lipstick.

"Pardon me while I hide in Ms. Johar's office," Tank said. "I may be in there a while, so don't go looking for me. I'd really rather not be on television.

You never know who might see you, and that's a chance I'd rather not take."

Huck watched as doors flew upon simultaneously on all sides of the van, and crew members hustled out, each to some specific duty. From the sliding side door, two hirsute young men in military surplus coats and wearing Eyewitness News caps hopped out as soon as the van came to rest. They began unpacking and assembling umbrella lighting, a long-armed audio boom, and a widescreen digital video camera. Working with practiced alacrity, they carried on some unintelligible conversation that involved frequent use of the words "dude," "tubular," and "gnarly," but which seemed unrelated to what they were doing.

A woman wearing a down parka with a fur-lined hood pushed through the side-by-side doors at the rear of the van, and once outside, climbed halfway up an aluminum ladder until she reached a crank, which she turned and, with great huffing and clouds of steam, raised the satellite dish on the roof. Once the dish was fully erect, she grabbed a handful of corkscrew cables dangling from its shaft and went back inside the van, closing the doors behind her.

Finally, from the front passenger side door, D'Nisha Glint stepped out carefully, testing her high-heeled footing on the icy surface of the parking lot.

"Holy moly mother of Mary," Val gasped. "They sent *D'Nisha Glint*!"

"Is she somebody famous?" Ximena asked. "I never watch the news."

"Uh, she's like *only* the host of Good Day Columbus, not to mention a former Ohio State Fair Queen. She's been with all the hottest guys." Val took a deep breath. "She even dated Adam Erb!"

"I like her," Chavonne commented further, "'cause she reminds me of Beyonce."

Amid the frigidity of that day, D'Nisha Glint's face seemed to radiate its own warm, mocha-colored light. She wore a white, knitted beanie hat with a slender headband that exposed her smooth brow. Beneath her bright blue Eyewitness News blazer, she wore pleated, pinstriped slacks. Walking ahead of the two technicians, she allowed them to catch up, but tilted her head backwards slightly when talking to them, in a way that seemed to ensure that they remained half a step behind her.

Chavonne pushed Huck, urging, "Don't keep her waitin'. Don't say nothin' dumb. And don't forget to give us a shout out."

Huck opened the door for D'Nisha Glint.

Upon entering, she unbuttoned her coat and gave it to one of the technicians to hang up. She shook her shoulders and straightened the lapels of her jacket. "Are you Huck Carp?"

"Yeah."

"Is that your real name?"

"Yeah."

"And you're the person in charge?"

"I guess so."

Meanwhile, the technicians cordoned off a corner of the seating area and began setting up their equipment.

Across the room, the Bottom Dwellers launched into a mid-tempo version of *The Banana Boat Song*.

D'Nisha looked Huck up and down, as if assessing his photogenic qualities. "As I said when we spoke, we've received several Eyewitness Action Tips about this pay-it-forward streak here today. It's just the kind of uplifting holiday story that our viewers can't get enough of."

She made a rolling hand signal to the technicians and said to them, "Let's start with a head-to head, high key lights, then at about thirty seconds start pulling back to the drive-thru window."

She pivoted and called back to Chavonne, Ximena, and Val, who had turned their backs on customers at the service window and were watching in rapt attention.

"Hi, everybody," she said. "You're going to be on TV. Look busy, but most of all, look happy."

Finally, returning her attention to Huck, she asked, "Are you ready to do this?"

"Yeah, uh, I guess so." He could feel Chavonne, Ximena, and Val's stares burning on his back. "Do I, uh, look okay?"

"You look charming," D'Nisha said.

Huck wasn't sure what *charming* looked like, or if that was a good thing. He'd surprised himself by even asking, as if looks should matter. The lights were making him squint, and he was conscious of the boom microphone hovering above him like a vulture.

"Relax." Microphone to her breast, D'Nisha listened while the camera technician counted down three, two, one....

"Good afternoon, Columbus. This is D'Nisha Glint reporting on a heartwarming story that is unfolding right now on the north side of the city, at the Drip 'n' Donuts store on Cleveland Avenue, where since 6:00 AM there has been a continuous pay-it-forward chain of customers through the drive-thru. I'm here with Huck Carp, the store's manager. Tell me, Huck, how did this get started?"

She had given Huck advance notice of what she would ask, and although he'd invested a good deal of thought to how he was going to answer her, now that he was on the spot, he realized that all of his answers sounded dumb. "Uhhhhhh."

"Was there anything special about today?"

Worse than not knowing what to say, though, was saying nothing. Huck thought of how the day had begun, by turning the page on his Daily Worker calendar—it was always a hopeful act. He turned the page again, in his mind, and began speaking.

"No. It was really just another day, with nothing especially revolutionary about it. Still, I always start the day with the hope that something amazing is going to happen. I think that optimism is essential, especially in these difficult times, don't you?"

Judging from D'Nisha Glint's expression, she hadn't expected to be asked a question—one of her cheeks twitched involuntarily. Oddly, though, her hesitation emboldened Huck.

"Sometimes it only takes one person to perform a single small, random act of kindness to give everybody a reason to pause, to think, and to realize that the most natural response is to do something kind in return. We're all in this together, so if we all just stand up as one for what's right, those who would do otherwise don't have a chance. The numbers are on the side of goodness. Good deeds are free, and they're also extremely contagious. I think that's the very definition of freedom—the ability to choose between doing good and bad things."

The twitch spread to D'Nisha's other cheek. She parted her lips, as if preparing to respond, but Huck hadn't finished.

In the background, Edgar sang, "Day O! Daaaaay O!"

"Because the spark of goodness, once lit, quickly catches fire and soon becomes a blaze for passion, for justice, for equality, and for human rights. What's happening today is proof of that. Nobody asked any of these people to join this movement, but they've been coming here all day long, one after the other, each giving and receiving according to their needs and means. That's how all revolutions begin, in the heart."

"How long...?" D'Nisha Glint tried to jump in, but Huck continued without taking a breath.

"And don't forget my comrades in arms." Huck gestured broadly in the direction of Ximena, Chavonne, and Val, so that the camera followed his movement. "They've been here since 6:00 AM, and they stayed beyond the end of their shifts, because they can feel the power of what's happening and want to bear witness to it, too. They're part of history."

"Wow," was all that D'Nisha Glint could manage.

The Bottom Dwellers amped up the volume and harmonized, "Daylight come and we wanna go home...." Customers in the shop started swaying, arms above their heads.

"So, let's all say it, shout it, sing it." Huck held out his fist and opened one finger, two fingers, three...

Chavonne, Ximena, and Val joined him, shouting, "Feed the Deed!"

"And get well soon, Wanda Pfaff," Chavonne interjected.

D'Nisha Glint kicked the camera technician to divert his attention back to her.

"Well, good luck with that," she said to Huck.

The segment finished with a cut-away shot at the drive-thru, where D'Nisha Glint interviewed a customer as he pulled up to the service window. By obvious design, the driver of that vehicle turned out to be the station's weatherman, who flashed thumbs-up while ordering two chocolate éclairs and a passion fruit smoothie for the next person in line. As he drove off, D'Nisha faced the camera, took a bite out of an éclair, an intoned, "D'Nisha Glint reporting for Eyewitness News."

"That's a wrap," she declared.

The whole episode took no more than twenty minutes, but to Huck, it divided ordinary from revolutionary time.

D'Nisha thanked him for being "enthusiastic" and wished him luck. Before leaving, upon Val's request, she consented to a group photo, where everybody wrapped their arms around the person next to them and kicked a leg in the air, like a chorus line.

"Did that really just happen, or did I dream it?" Val wondered aloud.

CHAPTER 12

3:30 PM

Adam Erb was enjoying himself so much that he bounced, heel to toe, while he worked. It felt as though he'd swallowed an effervescent tablet, which was tickling his spleen with kiss bubbles as it dissolved. This inner titillation inspired a little boogie in him, so he shimmied, he hummed, and he giggled continuously. He'd immersed himself entirely in a Drip 'n' Donuts persona, donning the company's baseball cap and pinning himself with a nametag, which read: *Adam ERB*, with his last name in all caps. He commandeered the drive-thru pickup window so that he, personally, greeted and bantered with every lucky customer before buying them a dozen donuts, with his sincere compliments. If he'd known that altruism was so much fun, he'd have done it earlier.

A gust tossed his hair as he slid open the window and accosted the next customer with, "Salutations and bon appetite. Today, I am going to make your day great."

The customer was driving a pickup truck with a gun rack. He spoke while chewing tobacco. "Yahr'll do what?"

"'Tis the season for giving, and nobody has the spirit more than me, Adam Erb. Perhaps you've heard. Today is my grand giveaway. Everybody gets a dozen free donuts. Merry Christmas, sir."

The man spit backwards, into the wind.

"A dozen donuts? Tha's twelve, raght?"

"Yessir. Just as there are twelve months, twelve disciples, and twelve steps, so too do donuts come in a dozen. And for you, sir, any twelve donuts are free of charge. That's my gift to you."

"Why for?"

"Because I'm paying-forward a random act of kindness."

Behind him, Phoebe gushed, "That's soooooo, like, sweet."

Adam winked at her.

"Did yahr jest wink at me?" the pickup driver asked defensively.

"Yes. Well, no, not at you. Not directly, at least. But I might as well have, because I'm doing you a favor. For free. That's worthy of a wink, maybe even a nod. So, which twelve donuts do you choose? They can be iced, glazed, sugared, filled with cream or jelly or chocolate, topped with sprinkles or nuts. What's your preference?"

"Large black coffee," the pickup truck driver said. "An' two plain cake donuts."

Adam looked back at Phoebe and rolled his eyes.

"Sir, that's excellent, but perhaps you didn't understand the nature of the gift that I am giving? You're eligible for not *two*, but *twelve* donuts. All that you have to do is choose any twelve. Feel free to mix and match. Compliments of Adam Erb."

"Ah cain't eat but two donuts."

"Of course. That's very frugal of you. But I reiterate that the twelve donuts are *free*. There's nothing to be gained by taking any less."

"Maybe yahr could give the extry t' th' next person in line?"

"No, no, no. That won't work, because I'm also giving that person twelve free donuts."

"So yahr'll give me twelve donuts, whether ah want them or not?"

"Yes sir. Now you get it."

"If so, give me a dozen plain cake donuts," the pickup truck driver said, then turned up the radio's volume on a Rascal Flatts song, thus ending the negotiation.

"You heard the man," Adam said to Phoebe, but before she could scamper away to fill the order, he grabbed her wrist, pulled her toward him, and whispered in her ear, "Throw in a couple of fancy donuts. That old hillbilly wouldn't know a good deal if it came with icing on top."

"Okay, Mr. Erb," Phoebe agreed.

When Adam handed the coffee and bag of donuts to the pickup truck driver, he started bouncing again. It amused him to think of the driver on the road, en-route to some filthy garage, mobile home, or redneck bar, then reaching into the bag expecting an ordinary donut, and pulling out a cheese Danish instead. At first, he might puzzle over it, maybe even pull over to ponder what it was and what had happened. Then, he'd take a bite, and hitherto unimagined sweetness would fill his mouth. Possibly, it might open his eyes to whole new worlds of confectionary possibilities. Adam counted it as yet another good deed done. This was cool. He was a philanthropist.

"Excuse me, Mr. Erb. You are very generous, but perhaps it would be better if you encouraged more customers to accept plain cake donuts, wherever possible."

Adam cringed. He didn't like the way those words seemed to masquerade bad news behind flattery.

"Who says?"

Ms. Doody kowtowed, while at the same time digging in her heels. "It's just that we have lots of plain cake donuts, but we're running out of other selections."

"That won't do," Adam complained. "Do I look like the kind of person who would make a gift of a plain cake donut to somebody?"

Ms. Doody looked him up and down, as if she was considering actually answering what Adam had intended, obviously, to be a rhetorical question.

"No, I don't," Adam answered. "That most certainly is *not* how I roll."

3:35 PM

Being an on-call limo driver meant having a lot of down time, just waiting for that call. While Adam Erb was busy serving donuts inside the Polaris Drip 'n' Donuts shop, Jay-Rome sat in the parking lot with the Hummer's heater on max, watching wind devils sweep falling and drifting snow into bizarre, undulating patterns. It was the finest snow that he'd ever seen, like fairy dust that flashed and glittered, forming brilliant streaks against the steely gray skies. It was mesmerizing.

Jay-Rome shook his shoulders and rubbed his eyes. There was no telling how long his boss might stick around the donut shop, because he was easily entertained and so long as peddling donuts continued to amuse him, he'd keep it up... but the moment that he decided the thrill had worn off, he'd want to hit the road out of there pronto. Jay-Rome had to be ready, in either case.

Looking for any diversion, he turned on the radio and flipped through station after station, until he heard the voice of his favorite news babe, D'Nisha Glint.

"Good afternoon. This is D'Nisha Glint reporting on a heartwarming story that is unfolding right now on the north side of the city, at the Drip 'n' Donuts store on Cleveland Avenue...."

Hot damn, Jay-Rome thought, *I wish I was there right now.* Picturing her in his mind made him wiggle in his Drawers.

"Damn," he muttered to himself. It bothered him that he'd missed D'Nisha Glint, just because his boss had gotten his feelings hurt and left in a huff. It always happened that way, though. He was always on call to go someplace where somebody else wanted to go, never where he himself wanted to be. He often fantasized about stretching out in the back of the limo in his silk pajamas with a fat blunt, a bottle of Mocato, and D'Nisha Glint on her knees in front of him, while Adam Erb, wearing one of those dumb, little boys' caps that chauffeurs wore, would call back to him, "Where to, Boss?"

On the radio, some kid with a puppy voice was talking happy bullshit. "We're all in this together."

'I wish that was true," Jay-Rome thought.

3:45 PM

Jack Gentile didn't need to be told to buckle his seat belt; it was already so tight that it cut into his gut. Nor did he appreciate hearing, "Taking off might be a little bumpy." He'd checked the weather forecast before deciding to board the plane, and it wasn't reassuring. Still, the pilot promised him that the weather would hold long enough to complete the short, half-hour flight to Columbus. At the same time, it unnerved him when she added, "But if it was an hour later, with this storm front moving in so fast, I'd be worried." A worried pilot is never a good thing, and it seemed to Jack that they had very little margin for error.

To remind himself of the importance of this impromptu business trip, he took out his cell phone and re-watched the You Tube video for the fourth time—a pirated clip of a story scheduled for airing on Eyewitness TV news at 5:00 PM that evening. It looked like it'd been recorded surreptitiously from a palmed hand, held at hip level, and although it jumped a lot and wasn't entirely intelligible, one things was clear to him: whatever was happening down there at the Cleveland Avenue store in Columbus, it was now a news story. If Drip 'n' Donuts was in the news for any reason anywhere in his region, Jack Gentile had to be there, blizzard be damned.

When the video finished, Jack checked his email, his Twitter, his Instagram, and his recent voicemail. Adam Erb's name was prominent in all those venues. It figured that, one way or another, if there was a trending story in Columbus, Adam was going to insinuate himself into it. Grabbing the center of attention was Adam's forté. If there was no avoiding him, then Jack figured it would be easier on him if he got ahead of the situation. He speed-dialed Adam.

"Dude," Adam responded to the call.

"Hey, A-man. I'm on my way to Columbus. I need to see what's going on there for myself."

Adam's voice jumped an octave. "No shit! That's great news. What's happening here is pretty special, if I do say so myself."

"Huh? Where are you? What are you doing?"

"Don't mess with me, dude. Why else would you be calling me?"

A good question, for which Jack had no immediate answer. "Do you have any idea what I'm talking about?" he asked plainly.

"My pay-it-forward."

"*Your* pay-it-forward?"

"Well, not literally and exclusively mine, but, yeah, I guess, it really is all about me. And it has been going strong for nearly two hours now."

"Only two hours? According to that kid on the video, Huck, it's been going on since six o'clock this morning."

"Pay no attention to that Huck person!" Adam snapped, so harshly that it felt to Jack like he'd just bitten off his earlobe through the phone. "As far as I'm concerned, those cretins at the Cleveland Avenue store lost all credibility when they refused my gift."

"Yeah, but... you haven't seen the video, have you? D'Nisha Glint did a report with Huck and the whole staff at Cleveland Avenue. It's already been on the radio and the internet, and it's going to be on the TV news this evening."

"D'Nisha? *My* D'Nisha?" Adam paused, as if giving this revelation time to sink in. "Fuck her, the vindictive bitch," Adam said when it did.

"Look, Adam, I have to go there to see what's going down. It's my job. Although, to be honest, I'm not sure what I'll do once I get there. The regular manager seems to have abandoned the store, and the staff are now running the show. I may need to take control. Still, with all the good publicity they're getting, I have to act like I approve of what they're doing. I really don't know how I'll handle this. They won't talk to me. I tried calling, but Huck, whoever the hell he is, insists that everything is okay and not to worry. He says he's doing the will of the people, whatever that means."

Adam said, "Hey, Jack ol' buddy," in the tone that Jack had come to recognize as prelude to calling in a favor. "Ignore those Commie assholes in Linden. It will end badly for them. Believe me. Instead, meet me here at the Polaris store. We've got our own bigger, better, more generous streak going. This is where you really want to be. Trust me."

Sudden turbulence walloped the plane. It felt to Jack like his head and his bowels were separated by about 5000 feet of altitude.

"Okay, okay, okay. I give. I'm landing in twenty minutes at the Ohio State University airport. It's close to you, so I can swing by on my way to Linden."

"Attaboy, Jack."

"Yeah."

Jack Gentile hung up, reflecting on how approval from Adam Erb often sounded like praise given from a master to his dog.

CHAPTER 13

3:50 PM

"¡*Mamá!* You are famous!" Tatiana cried.

Ignacio and Babette rushed past their sister straight to Ximena, and nearly bowled her over hugging her legs while she was delivering an order to a customer.

"Donuts, *por favor*," they pleaded.

"How cute," the customer said. "Enjoy them while they're little, because before you know it, they'll become *teenagers*."

"Hey!" Tatiana objected.

As soon as the customer had pulled away, Ximena said, "Never mind such fools. Today, we are happy."

"This is an amazing thing, *mamá*, what you are doing here today. As far as Facebook is concerned, there is nothing bigger happening in all of Columbus. This is *the* place to be. Friends have texted me, saying: *Tati, doesn't your mother work at that Drip 'n' Donuts where they got that streak thing going?* And I tell them that, yes, you do, and you have been there from the very beginning. All of my friends are jealous."

Ximena was pleased by Tatiana's approval, even if it did seem rather fickle. She tested the extent of that support by wrapping her arms around her daughter, who hugged her back. It felt like a moment made for memories.

While stroking Tatiana's hair with one hand, she waved at Val with the other. "Could you mind the window for a few minutes?" she asked.

Val smiled and nodded, seeming glad to have been asked.

"Come, children, I want to tell you something."

Gathering her children in the same spot where earlier D'Nisha Glint had interviewed Huck, she pulled up chairs and told them to sit.

"Do you want donuts? *Bueno.* But what about muffins, instead? We are running short of some donuts."

Huck brought three grape jelly donuts and handed one to each of Ximena's children. "We have enough for our special guests," he said, then left.

"Very well, so," Ximena began. "I want to tell you a story. Tati, you may remember it, because your *papa* told it to you when you were very little. In truth, I believe that he sent this memory to me straight down from heaven today. This is the story of Pepita, the poor little flower girl."

"I do remember. It's a Christmas story."

"*Si.* Pepita was a young girl who lived in a village where most people were very poor, except for the rich landlords who owned the farms where they all worked. One year at Christmas, the wealthy families built a glorious nativity scene on the town square. The baby Jesus lay in a bed made of pure gold. The rich children came bearing gifts of fruits and spices, beautiful piñatas, brilliant luminarias and such things that the poor children could only dream of, and they spread these fine gifts out before the baby Jesus.

"Pepita and the other poor children watched in sadness, for they had no such wonderful things to give the Lord. But Pepita wanted very much to get close to the baby Jesus, so she snatched up a handful of weeds from the roadside and took them to him, placing them at his feet, and there she knelt in prayer.

"And instantly the weeds turned into beautiful red star flowers! Poinsettias, *la flor de Nochebuena*. All the weeds along the roadside turned into poinsettias, too, so the other poor children could pick them and bring them to the baby Jesus. The nativity scene became a beautiful bouquet, thanks to Pepita, because even the most humble gift, if given with love, is a thing of true beauty."

Babette started crying. "I want to be like Pepita," she sniffed.

"But so you are, just like her. And so are you, Ignacio. And Tati. Because you have come here, to be a part of the giving chain of people paying-forward their gifts of love from one to another. Please remember this story, always, and remember, too, this day."

"*Mamá!*" Tatiana cried. "You tell the story even more beautiful than *Papa*."

"If you think so," Ximena said, "it is because he gave us the story, to pass to you, and so some day you may pay-it-forward, when you have your own *niños*."

Ximena lifted her head, and with that slight gesture created room for the three children to enter under her arms and fuse with her in an intimate embrace worthy of paying-it-forward.

3:55 PM

Val took a picture of Ximena and her kids hugging each other and immediately uploaded it into Facebook and Instagram, with the caption, "The true meaning of Christmas." The first "likes" appeared within seconds.

Being "liked" validated her. She was "friends" with and "followed" by many people whom she knew only in passing, or not at all in the real world, but whose approval she cultivated and appreciated in social media.

Sometimes, her mother scolded her, saying, "If you put half as much effort into real relationships — into finding a man, or, hell, a woman, I don't care — you'd be much happier."

It didn't matter how often Val assured her mother that she was, in fact, happy. The old lady just didn't get it. She was hopelessly analog.

Val enjoyed working the service window. Usually, she got stuck doing front counter duty, which, ironically, was far less interactive than the drive-thru. People who bought their donuts over-the-counter and stayed on the premises to eat them tended to avoid eye contact when ordering, and then retreated to some far corner where they ate in silent isolation. She suspected that they came because, for the admission price of just one plain donut, they could stay and sit, brood, dream, doze, or use the wifi for as long as they wished. Most of the time, if they spoke to her at all, it was to complain about something.

By contrast, folks passing by in the drive-thru seemed to understand that the success of their whole transaction required cooperation. They made a conscious effort to articulate when placing their orders over the intercom. They seemed genuinely thankful when they received correct orders, as if it always came as a surprise that the system had worked.

Val liked facilitating their gratitude. For some reason, though, despite her oft-expressed wish for more variety in her job, Ms. Johar seldom scheduled her to work the drive-thru. Instead, Ximena, Chavonne, and Wanda Pfaff — when she deigned to show up at all—always got the best jobs. And Huck... well, he was always willing to do anything for the "team," but sometimes he treated Val like a child, too. All she really wanted was a chance to prove herself.

Maybe today was that chance. The team needed her to step up, and she was determined not to blow it. To preserve a formal record of the day and of her contributions to it, she kept her cell phone next to her, and whenever something special happened, she took photos or videos, which she eagerly shared with her entire network of online friends, followers, lurkers, and everybody else with whom she had an internet-based relationship.

Normally, she ignored Chavonne or Ximena when they tsk-ed at her or mumbled to themselves that her social media activity was "a waste of time," but on that day, she felt vindicated, because this much Val knew for sure: if it wasn't for her, the good news about paying-it-forward would never have gone viral. Her tweets had been instrumental in creating the miracle. Even if they didn't understand her social media obsession, Val believed that her colleagues had to give her credit for that much.

Every time she received a new message or notification, her cell phone sounded a birdcall to alert her.

"'Sup, girl? Yo' cell phone sounds like a damn rainforest, so many birds," Chavonne remarked.

"Thank you, I guess."

"Who all sends yo' so much stuff, anyway? Do yo' really got that many friends?"

"Oh yes. I have over 1000 friends and 500 followers. I post something for them every single day, and so do they, so we all share, respond, react, and share some more."

"Uh huh." Chavonne took an order over the intercom.

Val thought that was probably the end of the subject, but Chavonne picked it up again a few seconds later.

"With all them friends and followers, don't yo' worry who they are and what they be doin' with all the information that yo' give up for free?"

"No, I don't worry. Why should I?"

"Girl, if yo' was black, yo' wouldn't have to ask that question."

Val didn't see what being black or white had to do with the matter. Still, she wasn't about to disagree with Chavonne about anything related to being black. That would be way sooooo politically incorrect.

"I guess," Val said in a sort of reply.

Chavonne didn't let the matter drop. "Ain't no question about it. Every little click or post or look online at gets logged into the records on some great big honkin' supercomputer. They call it *data*. They can use it to figure of what yo' like, where yo' live, who yo' spend time with, and other things that yo' don't even know about yo' own self. It's all for mind control."

"Who are they?"

"They is the gov'ment. The po-lice. The media. They doin' experiments. Ain't yo' ne'er heard of Tuskegee? Some of yo' so-called friends might actually be stealin' yo' data."

"No, I trust my friends and followers."

"Why for? How many of them have yo' ever had a real conversation with?"

Val paused, wondering if she should take offense. She considered not answering but caught herself saying, "Conversation is overrated."

"Ain't so," Chavonne retorted. "We is havin' us a conversation right now. It ain't been but a few minutes long, but I already learned more about yo' than I did in the whole six months what we've been workin' together."

"Yeah. Don't get me wrong. I like *real* people, too." Birdsong triggered a new thought process. "But. Well. Listen. It's like this...."

"I believe that anytime you're honest and share what you're thinking, feeling, and doing, whether it's with a flesh and blood human being or with hundreds of your friends on a digital distribution list, you make yourself vulnerable. People can take advantage of your honesty, but I think it's a chance worth taking. There's no perfectly safe way to open yourself up to another person. But when somebody else out there relates to what you're thinking, feeling or doing, and they acknowledge it, it doesn't matter whether they are right next to you or out there in digital space. You've made a connection. And when enough of those people find each other, they can make things happen all at once, from the ground up, that wouldn't ever happen any way otherwise. Things like paying-it-forward."

Chavonne removed her earphones, as if to let those words sink in deeper. "Maybe," she said. "I can't say that I don't agree."

To Val, that sounded like she was being "liked."

4:15 PM

"We just sold out of Boston Crème donuts," Ximena shouted at Huck.

"Oh, shit," Huck said.

Sitting at Ms. Johar's desk, he'd been double checking the morning's delivery statement against on-hand inventory and the current pace of sales for each item. By his reckoning, if the afternoon delivery, which was already late, didn't arrive within the hour, they'd be down to Dripkins, flatbreads, and that awful Chai tea that nobody ever drank. Huck flipped through Ms. Johar's rolodex, looking for contact information on the distributor, so he could call for a status report.

Edgar entered the office without knocking. Although normally rather flamboyant, Edgar could be surprisingly furtive, too. Huck had no idea how long he'd been watching before he noticed him standing there.

"Look at you, Huckster. If you were wearing a suit and tie, I'd say that you look just like a regular businessman."

"No need to be insulting, Edgar. I'm just doing the best I can."

"And you are doing fan-fucking-tastic. Really. I'm in awe of what you've accomplished here. People are coming from all over the city to jump on board the peace train. Ooh-wah-ee-wah-ooh-gah."

"Eh?

"Never mind. I got carried away." Edgar pulled the door shut behind him. He grinned that smarmy grin of his. "There's something about a revolution that makes me horny."

Head down, Huck winced. That disclosure, however untimely, was hardly surprising—if there was air in the room, Edgar was horny. Sexual adventurism was part of his personal philosophy. Chapter two of his manifesto was entitled "Sex after Capitalism," and it included copious references to Marx, Wilhelm Reich,

Immanuel Kant, Alfred Kinsey, Oscar Wilde, Doctor Ruth, and Ru Paul. Huck had read it, so it wasn't like he didn't know what he was getting into. For Huck, consenting to sex with Edgar was more of an intellectual than a hormonal impulse. He believed it was important for any open-minded, 21st century progressive to give homosexuality a fair trial. Still, it bothered Huck that the last time Edgar fellated him, his mind had been full of visions and fantasies of Edgar's sister, not Edgar himself. It seemed impolite.

"Uh, well...." Huck sputtered.

Edgar swept aside the papers and files on the desk and slid across, writhing his hips so as to feature the tumescence in his trousers. "What do you say to a quickie?"

"Whoa, Edgar. Really? Now is not a good time."

"I know. That's what makes it sexy."

"Naw. I mean, thanks for thinking of me, but I'm really busy."

"You're stressed." Edgar reached for Huck's crotch. "I know just the thing to fix that."

Huck swatted Edgar's hand... emphatically.

"Hey! You just about broke my wrist. What's wrong with you?"

"Sorry, but I'm worried. This is too important. I can't let it fail."

"How would a quick hand job hurt?"

"I'm just not in the mood, Edgar."

"Ouch!" Edgar jumped off the table. "I get the message. But, shit, Huck—what's come over you?"

"Please leave. I have to make some phone calls."

"Okay, okay, okay. Be that way. Don't mind me. I'll just have to go to the restroom and take care of my own needs."

"Go!"

Edgar paused in the doorway on the way out. "I'll be fine."

"Go. *Now!*"

Alone, Huck counted to ten, then when he was fairly sure that Edgar wasn't coming back, he sighed as deeply as if he'd been underwater for ten minutes. Probably, Edgar was already masturbating in a restroom stall, or maybe he was hitting on some more agreeable partner. If so, Huck was relieved to be cheated on. He had work to do.

He couldn't figure out who to call for a status report on the afternoon delivery. Ms. Johar's rolodex contained numerous cards indexed with the names and contact information for what seemed like everybody that she'd so much as shaken hands with over the last decade. Included among them were several cards for shipping, trucking, transportation, and delivery services, any of which might be responsible for bringing the afternoon shipment. He wished that he'd paid more attention to such things, but he'd never previously imagined any scenario where they'd matter to him. Lacking any better strategy, he started making calls, beginning with the A's, using the same script each time.

"Hello, this is Huck Carp, interim manager of the Cleveland Avenue Drip 'n' Donuts in Columbus. I'm calling to inquire about the status of our afternoon delivery."

He made it to the M's before getting an affirmative response. "Yes, sir, we subcontract with Drip 'n' Donuts for deliveries," the raspy voice on the phone said. "But I don't understand why you're asking. The afternoon delivery to Cleveland Avenue was cancelled two hours ago."

Huck felt his lungs deflate. "That's impossible."

"The note says that the order was cancelled in it's entirely by Uma Johar."

"Oh my god. Can I reverse that decision? We do need that order. We need it very much."

"Sorry, sir, but even if I wanted to, I couldn't at this late hour. The weather has wreaked havoc with our schedule. But Merry Christmas, anyway."

Huck dropped the phone and buried his head in his hands. Angst and despair swarmed his thoughts, but at the same time, he felt a slow rage boiling in his chest. One by one, he started knocking things off Ms. Johar's bookshelf — her stapler, her tape dispenser, her mini-fan, her Shiva dancing figurine, the photo of her cat....

"Fuck you, Johar!" he shouted, spittle flinging from his mouth. He wished that she could've been there to hear him.

That capitalist bitch!

She'd apparently decided that if she was going down, she would take everybody else down with her. Huck ripped Ms. Johar's framed diploma off the wall and hurled it like a Frisbee out the office door. It landed in a bus tray full of dirty dishes and shattered dramatically.

The Bottom Dwellers stopped playing in the middle of a tune. Voices hushed.

Huck felt the edgy silence engulf him like being swallowed, then spit back out. He knew it was his duty to break the bad news to everybody, and figured he'd better do it now, while still pissed, or else he might break down and start crying.

CHAPTER 14

4:32 PM

Huck stepped out of Ms. Johar's office, clapped his hands, and called at the top of his lungs, "Listen up!"

The crowd ceased all song, chatter, banter, and merriment immediately. Huck was aware of all eyes following him as he rounded the counter, walked to the center of the floor, and opened his arms as if to gather everybody's attention. His thoughts sped through a dizzy succession.

What's going on? Who are these people? What do they want from me?

He hopped onto a chair so that he could see their faces. This was a perspective that he'd never sought: elevated, commanding the public's regard, looked upon by them for guidance and purpose. He felt like an imposter.

The shop had filled with many more people. Some of them were familiar, the usual riffraff and groupies that followed the Bottom Dwellers wherever they went. Most of them, though, were newcomers who'd arrived as strangers but now seemed to have been integrated into the fellowship of streakers. For all the energy emanating from the crowd, though, Huck felt exposed, a naked emperor, inadequate to the task he was called upon to do. He'd never wanted to be a leader of anything, and he especially abhorred being the bearer of bad news.

Tank sidled next to him. "It's gonna be okay, kid."

"Really? Do you really think so?" Huck retorted. He wouldn't have expected feel-good platitudes from Tank, of all people. "No!" He found himself amplifying, facing Tank but speaking to the masses. "I'm tired of believing that everything is going to be *okay*. Saying that is neither comforting nor encouraging, when it's obviously not true. The truth is that we got screwed by the powers that be. Just like always."

He lifted his chin and turned to the crowd. "Earlier this afternoon, the manager of this store fled because she couldn't control the will of the people, and when she saw the power of our movement, which terrified her. Before she left, though, she did what authority always does when it feels threatened. She sabotaged us. She cancelled the afternoon delivery."

Gasps and moans ensued, followed by boos. Somebody cried, "Why?"

Tank bent closer to Huck and spoke into his ear. "Nice speech, kid, but it is really gonna to be okay. Just listen to me."

Huck noticed a rolling pin on a shelf beneath the counter. He grabbed it and brandished it above his head. "I won't lie to you, comrades. Our situation is grim. We've already run out of several menu items, and when the last of the donuts is gone, we'll be left with nothing but our ideals and good intentions to pay-forward. I don't know how much longer we can hold out."

The crowd responded with a rolling cascade of "Noooooo," with individual voices calling out "Bastards!" and "Fuckers!" as well as chants of "Get up!" and "Fight back!"

The cries drowned out Tank, whose lips were moving, but Huck could not hear the words coming out of his mouth.

Rolling pin in one hand, the other a clenched fist, Huck shouted, "But we can't be stopped! We'll pay-it-forward in justice! What do we want?"

"Justice!"

"When do we want it?"

"Now!"

And so it went on for several cycles. Huck absorbed each echoing response like pulses of pure passion, zapped straight into his soul—not that he believed he had an actual soul, for as an atheist, he did not, but never matter, because divine or not, at that moment, some kind of spiritual substance possessed him. The group's affirmations intensified his righteous indignation, as well as his confidence. He imagined that he felt how Martin Luther King, Jr. must have felt at the Lincoln Memorial in 1963. Every time he raised his arm holding the rolling pin, he was answered by another roar for justice.

He wondered how long he could keep it up.

When he heard horns honking outside, Huck assumed that the chant had spread to the drivers in the pay-it-forward line, and honking was their way of joining in. It gradually dawned on him, however, that one horn was exceptionally loud—a trucker's air horn—and it was out of synch with the cadence. It seemed to be saying *get out of my way.*

Some folks in the store noticed, too. They turned to look, pressing their hands and faces against the plane glass windows to see outside. Others swarmed outside, into the frigid cold. Amid the honking and chanting, the sound of a cheer began to rise.

Huck dashed outside, shielding his eyes from the pounding snow. Through the blur and the din, he perceived a small vehicle with flashing blue and red emergency lights on its roof, and it was being followed by a large truck with Christmas tree lights strung along its cab and on its sides. The truck driver blasted the air horn repeatedly, as if out of sheer joy. Huck squinted, rubbed his eyes, and was finally able to make out that Flubber Fusco was piloting his mall security golf cart, like a tugboat leading a food service delivery truck through the pay-it-forward line, toward the loading dock where dozens of people had assembled to welcome it.

"What the fuck?" Huck asked aloud, to nobody in particular.

Tank, who had followed him out the door, answered, "I tried to tell yah, kid. C'mon."

Tank dragged Huck by the sleeve to the loading dock. When the truck backed into the bay, Tank threw open its lift gate. Inside were crates loaded with donuts, breads, eggs, drink mixes, and assorted frozen foodstuff. Using hand signals, Tank organized a human chain for unloading. The whole time, traffic through the pay-it-forward line never missed a beat.

Scooter Opalinsky hopped out of the truck's cab and waved at Huck. "Sorry that I couldn't get here sooner," he said. "But the roads are like an ice rink."

4:55 PM

Huck, Tank, and Scooter were in Ms. Johar's office, passing a joint. The truck had been unloaded, the delivery checked, and the inventory re-stocked, all accomplished by voluntary group efforts from folks who sang *Solidarity Forever* while passing boxes hand to hand. Though uplifting, it also baffled Huck. Revolutions were supposed to be messier. The pay-it-forward streak was up to 392 consecutive customers, and now, thanks to the unexpected delivery, it looked as though they could maintain it all night, if luck and goodwill held.

Finally, there was time for Huck to ask, "How?"

Scooter bogarted the joint while telling his story. "I've been following the pay-it-forward ever since I got my first morning tweet on the subject. I admit that I was a little jealous, to tell the truth. It didn't seem fair that something so special should happen here while I was off duty. But as the day wore on and the streak lasted, I began to hope that it'd still be going when my shift started. I figured that, possibly, I might even be on duty when we broke the record. Then, early in the afternoon, I got a call from Tank."

"Tank?"

"Don't look so shocked," Tank said, leaning back in Ms. Johar's ergonomic chair. "I had a bad feeling about how old lady Johar left today, sneaking out like a crook and a coward. I figured she was hiding something. While you were doing your reality show with the TV people, I did some checking, and I discovered that she'd cancelled the whole afternoon delivery. So, I thought it through and got an idea, which I figured might work, although, technically, it involves grand larceny, sort of."

"No sort of about it," Scooter corrected him. "To those assholes at the Polaris store, it will most assuredly be considered grand larceny. It couldn't happen to a more deserving bunch, too. They're totally stuck up, like their shit don't stink."

Huck shook his head. "What does Polaris have to do with it?"

Tank smiled. "We stole their afternoon delivery."

Huck stared for just a second. "You did not!"

Scooter said, "Yes, we did! It was easy, too. I got my start at Drip 'n' Donuts driving the afternoon delivery truck. So, when Tank told me what happened, I called the distributor and offered to do the delivery myself. He knew me, so he didn't think twice. In fact, he was grateful, because as it turned out, one of his drivers called in sick and he didn't have anybody to take the route. He said that my offer was a Christmas miracle."

"Praise the Lord," Tank said.

Huck whistled in admiration. He'd always believed in civil disobedience as a moral tool for combatting injustice, but the idea of stealing a delivery truck was definitely ballsy. He wondered if he was in any way culpable. He kind of hoped so, because he wanted to take some credit for it. If anybody was going to jail for the cause, it should be him.

"I have to hand it to you guys," Huck said. "We've got some quality nonviolent resistance going on here, mixed in with a bit of redistribution of capital. To quote Eugene Debs: 'Only the working class can emancipate the working class.' This is starting to look like a real revolution."

"Save your dime store philosophy for bathroom stalls, kid," Tank admonished him. "I just want to see how far we can take this."

CHAPTER 15

5:07 PM

Jay-Rome eased into sleep. With the limo idling, the seat warmer radiating gentle warmth onto his posterior, radio 98.5 playing smooth jazz through surround sound speakers, and absolutely nothing in the world that he had to do, staying awake seemed like a waste of time.

A rappiing on the window jerked Jay-Rome out of his pleasant reveries. He'd been dreaming of blizzard-driven snow melting into crystal pools around D'nisha Glint's nude body—the best sex dream... ever, and getting better. He closed his eyes tighter and recoiled around the dream, trying to hang on, but the rapping got louder, like a headache intruding on a happy thought. Finally, the dream vision popped like a bubble, leaving Jay-Rome with no choice but to wake up.

Somebody was standing outside the drivers' side window, clutching his coat by its lapels with one hand and gesturing for Jay-Rome to roll down the window with the other.

Jay-Rome cracked the window and called, "Who's there?"

"Hey, nigga, I caught yo' slumpin' on the job," Clarence Bone said. "If I did that, my ass would get fired yesterday."

Jay-Rome reached across the front seat to open the door. "Get in here. It'll freeze yore nips out there."

He and Clarence knew each other from the limo service that employed them both. They'd been known to knock off a couple of Olde English 800s together from time to time, although it'd been a few months since they'd seen each other.

Clarence slid into the passenger seat after engaging in a brief tug-of-war with the wind to close the door. "Damn straight. It's so cold that my asshole's froze shut," he said, breathing heavily.

"That's what for I've got the heater chuggin' on the max. The boss man stashed me here while he's busy chasin' clout with the donut geeks on the inside. He's gettin' off on some kinda crusade."

Clarence laughed. "That's lamzy, man. I think our two bosses are tryin' to out-asshole each other. Mine just flew down from Toledo, even in this brick weather. What for? I don't know. I don't care. If yo' can 'xplain rich white people to me, yo'd be the first."

"I guess that leaves us with nothin' to do but chillax in our Hummers."

"That's wicked, man. Got any weed?"

"Naw, but maybe some Bud Light in the back."

Jack Gentile had seen his old pal Adam Erb in a many roles, guises, and personas, going back to their days as Beta Theta Pi fraternity brothers at Case Western Reserve University. He'd seen Adam in a white sheet toga and in a Versace suit. He'd seen him on his knees sloppy drunk in front of a gas station toilet, and he'd seen him in the spotlight on stage delivering a motivational speech for thousands. For all the times, places, and manners that he'd personally experienced Adam Erb's charisma, though, he never would have thought that he'd see him wearing a white apron over a candy-striped Drip 'n' Donuts shirt, with a Drip 'n' Donuts baseball cap on his head, and a name tag pinned above his heart identifying him as "Adam ERB," while he intoned, "How can I make your day great?"

It was shocking, kind of sickening, and seemed extremely out of character.

Upon seeing Jack, Adam crossed his arms and demanded, "What took you so long?"

Irked by Adam's tone, Jack masked his ambivalence by giving Adam a big man hug. "I got here as soon as I could."

"Yeah, sure." Adam wiped his hands on the apron. "I'm just anxious."

"Why?"

"Just look...." Adam stepped aside and gestured for Jack to behold. "What I started here is truly remarkable. So far, I've bought donuts for 38 consecutive customers. People are loving it like crazy. Now *that's* what I call paying-it-forward."

"That's great. Really."

"Listen to me, Jack. This here is the real pay-it-forward story that you want to get behind, not whatever the hell kind of bohemian, Kumbaya-singing, Woodstock-with-donuts-love-fest they're having down at Cleveland Avenue. It'll fizzle out like it never happened, but here we're doing solid good works, like Mother Theresa."

"Mother Theresa?"

"Absolutely... if she'd been fully capitalized, that is. What I'm doing is a charitable act. I consider myself an altruist."

"An altruist?"

"Well, maybe more of a philanthropist. I think this might be tax deductible."

Whether Adam considered himself to be an altruist, a philanthropist, or Santa Claus didn't matter to Jack. The larger issue to him was: *What the hell am I doing here?*

He opened a recent Instagram posting on his cell phone and showed it to Adam. "Have you seen this?"

The posting showed a short, jumbly video of a throng of people assembled outside the Cleveland Avenue Drip 'n' Donuts, cheering the arrival of a delivery truck. It showed Huck waving a rolling pin and shouting, "Liberty! Equality! Fraternity!"

"Huh?" Adam snatched the cell phone out of Jack's hand. "What the hell is this?" He expanded a section of the screen to better examine the exhilaration on Huck's face. "God-fucking-damn them to bloody hell. How is this possible?"

Adam tossed the phone back to Jack and called, "Ms. Doody, come here!"

Ms. Doody appeared from her office, and appeared startled when she saw Jack. "Oh my! When did you arrive, Mr. Gentile?"

Adam snapped his fingers in front of her face. "Over here, please. I don't understand what's happening. How did Cleveland Avenue get its delivery, when we're still waiting for ours?"

Ms. Doody blinked rapidly, like windshield wipers in a storm.

"Would you please look into that matter for me?" Jack asked.

"Yes, sir. Thank you, sir. Of course. I will make some calls and get to the bottom of this."

"See that you do," Adam said, getting the last word.

During the interlude, while Adam left the service window to confer with Jack, Phoebe and Pandora had stepped up to keep the flow of drive-thru business moving.

Adam pointed them out to Jack. "Look at those two, hopping around like rabbits, so full of energy and eager to help. Do you know what I appreciate the most about them?"

Jack was almost afraid to ask, so he shrugged.

"Their loyalty!"

"What are you talking about? Loyalty to Drip 'n' Donuts? Hell, I'm the regional manager, and I'm loyal to the company only so far as my next paycheck. No job is worth your loyalty, because no job will be loyal to you. It's just business, Adam. You know that."

"I meant loyalty to *me*."

"Pardon me, Adam, but that's even more absurd. Do they even know you?"

"No, thank God, but I know them." Adam took out his cell phone, opened his Facebook profile page, clicked on "friends," and began scrolling. "These are my Erb-ites—my friends, followers, freaks, and fanatics. Every day, legions of them begin their days by looking to me for guidance. They hearken to my every posting and tweet, share and discuss every blurb, as if whatever drivel I post is the eleventh commandment given to me by Jesus on Mount Sinai."

"You mean Moses."

"No, actually I think that I have more in common with Jesus. When I'm walking down any busy sidewalk in Columbus, I can tell just by looking at them which passersby are my followers. I see their glances, hear their whispers. Sometimes, if so inspired, I'll go out of my way to accost them, introducing myself by saying,

'I'm Adam Erb, and I just wanted to say hello.' They blush. They swoon. They gush. They fawn all over me. They say it's an honor to meet me. If they ask for a selfie, I say it would be my distinct pleasure, and you should see the expression of utter, unmitigated love on their faces. It's almost like being worshipped."

Adam shook his head. "Don't look at me like that! If they looked at you that way, you'd know what I'm talking about."

If Jack had looked at Adam in any way that suggested doubt or incredulity, it was an accident. If he felt anything, it was pity. "Uh huh," he muttered. "Well, uh...."

At that moment, Ms. Doody emerged from the office, her face sagging. She met Adam and Jack's questioning expressions with a sniffle and sunken eyes. "I'm so sorry," she said, her voice cracking. "There was some kind of mistake. Something went wrong with the delivery."

"What did you do?" Adam demanded to know.

"I'm sure that it wasn't your fault," Jack said.

Ms. Doody placed a hand to her heart, as if swearing an oath. "I don't know what... I don't know how... but, somehow, for some reason, the order that was meant for us seems to have gotten diverted to Cleveland Avenue. One of my former employees works there now—he always was a troublemaker, that one. Apparently, he hijacked the delivery truck and drove it there instead of here."

Adam threw his hands up. "It was stolen!"

"So it would seem," Ms. Doody confirmed.

Adam stood, stiffened his shoulders, and hovered above Ms. Doody, who shrank beneath him. His breath fogged her glasses. At once, he erupted, letting go of a bellowing "*Fuck it all!*"

He kicked over a rack of muffin trays, which flew in several directions like shrapnel and sent the staff scrambling to get out of the way.

Phoebe backed up to the service window, as if prepared to jump out, and Pandora shielded herself behind the door to a walk-in cooler.

Adam ripped off his Drip 'n' Donuts shirt, snapping off its buttons, then tossed his cap onto the floor and began stomping on it.

The woman with a tear tattoo shed an actual tear.

"It's all fucking goddamned over!" he screamed. "No more donuts! No more streak! No more... *me!*"

Jack stepped between Adam and the store's intimidated staff. He reached toward him tentatively, as if expecting a kickback, until landing his hand on Adam's shoulder. "It's okay."

"Okay my *ass!*" Adam blurted. He wagged a finger in Jack's face. "This is not *fair!*"

"No, it's not."

"That was *my* shipment. Jack, you've got to do *something.*"

However irrational Adam's behavior, that was a valid point.

"Leave it to me," Jack said. "I'm going there to take care of business."

"I'm coming too!"

Jack knew that if he said no, Adam would follow him anyway. Besides, it seemed advisable to keep an eye on him.

"All right. We'll go in my vehicle."

"Sure. I'll send my driver back home. Let's go, now. You should call the cops."

"Maybe. I suppose that I might have to."

Adam grabbed his coat. "Let's roll."

CHAPTER 16

6:00 PM

The scene surrounding the Cleveland Avenue Drip 'n' Donuts of north Columbus looked like a bacchanalia had broken out in a war zone. Folks packed inside the store danced around and made merry. Pilgrims unable to squeeze inside massed on the sidewalk and patio, warming themselves against the blizzard around an array of garbage can fires that blazed like pyres at a pagan ritual. Nearly every vehicle navigating the ice and driven snow on Cleveland Avenue that evening was bound for the Drip 'n' Donuts, since any persons with common sense had hunkered down at home, safe from the storm. It was hard to see where the line for the drive-thru began, because it branched and snaked through alleys, side streets, and across the parking lot before converging at a juncture where Flubber Fusco had posted a stop sign. To advance beyond that point, drivers were on their honor to enter the main channel one at a time and in turn.

It was orderly chaos.

"This has got to stop," Adam Erb said. "It's dangerous."

"It might be," Jack agreed. "But it's also fucking amazing."

From their strategic vantage across Cleveland Avenue, parked in front of the dollar store, Adam and

Jack wiped the fog off the limo's window and gazed in astonishment. The were stunned by the magnitude of revelry and public fanfare, far beyond anything they'd expected. Their distance provided perspective and safety, but the spectacle was growing, swallowing everything in its path.

"What's the plan?" Adam asked.

"Not sure. I had intended to walk right in and talk to them. Now I'm having second thoughts. If I go in, I might not make it out alive."

"I told you to call the cops. You have a riot on your hands. They may have hostages. Who knows?"

"Let me think." Jack pinched the bridge of his nose. "I need something to drink. Reach into the cabinet behind you and grab the bottle of Hennesey VSOP. And two glasses."

When Jack unsealed the bottle, the fumes cleared his sinuses all the way to the back of his mouth. He poured three fingers into each of the glasses and handed one to Adam, who held his glass in front of him, suggestive of preparing to propose a toast. Jack drank as if in a hurry, quaffing his drink down in two gulps. He winced, then let out a "Whooo" and bugged his eyes, as if experiencing sudden bain freeze.

"Do you know what this reminds me of, Adam?"

Adam gulped to catch up. "The worst traffic jam of your life?"

"It reminds me of our undergraduate commencement ceremony."

"Really? I can't remember anything about it. Maybe that's because I was wasted on quaaludes and Jello vodka shots."

"Most of the ceremony is lost in memory fog for me, too, but some parts are as vivid in my mind as if they happened yesterday. It was an unusually hot day, as hot as today is cold. We were sitting in those rickety aluminum folding chairs on a tarp that had been placed over the gym floor. I remember waiting for what seemed like hours to hear my name called. I watched person after person walk across the stage, shake the fat man's hand, grab a piece of paper, then march away to make room for the next person... and the next person... and on and on. I remember thinking that all it would take to bring the whole, carefully coordinated production crashing down was for one person to do something out of the ordinary, whether selfish or subversive or even by mistake. It wouldn't matter, because once the flow was interrupted, nobody would know what to do to make things right again.

"I also remember thinking that it wasn't fair. That was supposed to be my moment of glory. I wanted more than half a second — when the fat man called my name — to bask in the glow, so I determined that I when my turn finally came, I was going to come to a full stop, turn, and shout out loud, *Boo Yah*.

"But I didn't. When I heard my name, I choked. I lost my nerve. I hardly even slowed down, just shook the old fucker's hand, grabbed that piece of paper, then scooted right down from the stage, as if swept away by a giant broom. When I got back to my seat, I looked at the paper, and instead of a diploma, it was just a stupid letter that said, *Congratulations Graduate*.

"And I have regretted what I didn't do ever since."

Adam rolled his eyes into his head, as if either trying to recall or trying to forget — Jack couldn't tell which.

"Snap out of it, Jack. We've got to do something."

"Not necessarily." Jack took the bottle from Adam and poured himself another shot. "We could sit here and get drunk, just watching and waiting for things to fall apart on their own. Or not. Whatever. It's Christmas, after all."

"Oh puh-lease," Adam groaned. "As if Christmas is any reason to let them rub shit in your face. Get real. You're looking at theft, fraud, insubordination, and god-only-knows what kind of potential liabilities. You *have* to call the cops." He took out his cell phone. "If you won't do it, I will."

"You're a real kill joy, Adam," Jack said. "No, it's my job, not yours. Just let me finish my drink first."

For that night, unofficial membership in the Bottom Dwellers expanded to include by default every musician who showed up at Drip 'n' Donuts with an instrument in hand and a desire to join in. To Huck, it looked like the entire population of street corner buskers and coffee shop minstrels in North Columbus had assembled. They included Laine McGuffey, Ozzie the Singing Cowboy, Gordo and Pistol Pete of the Flea Pickers, Azure Higgenbottom with her falsetto and autoharp, and four of the Five Guys Named Mo.

Somewhere amid the bedlam, Edgar had disappeared—probably off getting laid, Huck assumed, and was glad for it. In his absence, Eileen had taken over coordinating the session, although with its size and varied levels of musicianship, the only rule seemed to be that everybody should be playing approximately the same tune.

With Scooter Opalinsky on duty, for the first time since the streak started, Huck felt at liberty to have some fun. He'd played with the Bottom Dwellers on several occasions. Oh, he had no delusions about why Edgar invited him to play washboard with the band, the overture quite clearly intended more as foreplay than appreciation for his musical talent. Still, it had set a precedent that Huck expected to be honored, and he was eager to join in.

With no washboard handy, Huck grabbed the next most suitable homemade percussive utensil: a pair of stainless steel dinner spoons. He'd seen people playing the spoons before. How hard could it be? Grabbing them with one hand and slapping with the other, he began rattling the spoons against his lap during *The Old Plank Road*. It took him a while to get the hang of it. Once, the top spoon jumped out of his hand and bounced against the fret of Eileen's banjo. By the end of the song, though, Huck was convinced that he didn't sound half bad.

After finishing the tune, Eileen approached Huck and asked, "Who taught you to play those spoons?"

"Uh... Edgar."

"Well...." She seemed to hold back a ghost of a smile. "Let me show you an easier method." Maneuvering beside him, she took his hand. "Hold the top spoon in place with your thumb, and curl your pointer beneath it... like this."

Huck's fingers became paralyzed.

"Loosen up." She massaged his thumb muscles. "Your name is Huck, right?"

"Yeah."

"How do you know Edgar?"

In what sense of the word "know" is she speaking?

"We met in a sociology class at Ohio State."

"So, you're a student?"

"I dropped out. The costs of higher education are inflated by the controlling elite, so they can monopolize knowledge and thereby keep the masses in thrall."

"Really?" She turned over Huck's hand and began kneading his palm. "That sounds like something my brother would say."

Whatever she meant by that remark—if anything—it made Huck feel like he was on the spot to say something that was totally unlike anything that Edgar would say, to separate the two of them. Unfortunately, every thought in his head spoke to him in Edgar's voice.

Then, as if to rescue him, Tank called out, "Hey, boss."

Huck pivoted and returned a hearty, "You called?"

"I got somebody on the phone who wants to talk to you. He says it's urgent."

"Oh?" Huck liked the sound of that.

"Yeah, says his name is Jerk the Gentle Giant—or something like that. Anyway, he claims to be the regional manager of Drip 'n' Donuts. He asked for you by name."

Eileen let go of his hand. "You'd better go take that call, *boss*."

"Yeah, I guess I had better. It might be important." Huck put the spoons in his pocket. "But I'll be right back."

Huck accepted the phone from Scooter, and wondered how he should answer it. He'd never answered a phone in the capacity of somebody in authority. The standard "How can I make your day great?" seemed like a silly and servile way to take a call from the regional manager. "Hello" seemed too weak. "How can I help you?" felt too solicitous. And what did this person want with him, anyway? Maybe he should ask, instead, "What can you do for me?" If only he'd thought of it, he would've come up with a list of demands.

"Hello? Is this Huck?" the voice on the other end finally inquired.

"Yes, Huck Carp."

"And you're in charge?"

Much as he liked the sound of that, he replied, "I am the first among equals."

"I'm Jack Gentile, regional manager for Drip 'n' Donuts. I'm the person who is ultimately responsible for everything that happens in your store."

"You can't take credit for our revolution."

"Your *revolution*? Believe me, I have no desire to take credit for any part of it."

"That's where we differ, sir. I'm proud to have had a part in the awakening of communal spirit that has taken place here today among the working people on the north side of Columbus. I hope that it grows, spreads, flourishes."

"I get it. I really do. When I saw the segment on Eyewitness News, I thought to myself, 'that's kind of cool.' So, I decided right away to come here, to see for myself." Jack cleared his throat. "But that was before you stole a delivery truck. That was before you kicked out the store manager. That was before a mob took control of the store."

"The revolution is not an apple that falls when it is ripe. You have to make it fall."

"Che Guevara? You're quoting Che Guevara to me?"

This tested Huck's presumption that anybody conversant about Che Guevara was okay by him. He felt as though he'd been called out.

Jack continued. "Listen to me, Huck. I admire your idealism. Really, I do. I wish that I had more of it, myself." He sighed. "But it's gotten out of hand. You have to shut it down and disperse. Otherwise, I'll have no choice but to contact the authorities."

Any sympathy Huck had for Jack's point of view was shattered when he heard the word "authorities." That summoned images of a jack-booted SWAT team armed with automatic weapons, eager to herd them up and haul them away.

"Oh yeah. Well... up yours! Hell no, we won't go! Power to the people!"

With immense satisfaction, but also a quiver of anxiety, he hung up.

Jack braced himself for the next, inevitable words to assault him.

"I told you so," Adam said.

Given the opportunity to gloat, Adam's reaction was as predictable as the sunrise, almost as pitiful as it was annoying. Almost.

"Tell me, Adam. Why are you taking this so personally? Is it because you feel slighted? Cheated? Overshadowed? Because when you get right down to it, none of this has anything to do with you."

"Everything is personal."

Jack supposed that, to Adam, everything was.

"I had to give talking to him a try. It was the least I could do. But now, I suppose that, yeah, I have no choice but to call the cops. This could get ugly."

Adam snapped his fingers. "Wait just one minute. I have another idea."

"Does it involve weapons of mass destruction?"

"Shut up. Listen to me. I've been right so far...."

Jack was unwilling to either concede or challenge that point, so he let it slide.

"...So why don't you let me give my Plan B a shot?"

It wasn't so much a matter of being willing, as it was being out of better options.

Jack shrugged. "What have I got to lose?"

CHAPTER 17

6:18 PM

Val buzzed with energy, and wore a smile on her face that stretched from dimple to dimple. She cheerfully multitasked at the service window: filling orders, ringing up transactions, schmoozing with streakers, while always remaining vigilant to her cell phone for the latest incoming chatter. In between customers, a new message in all caps seized her attention—a text message from ADAM ERB. She felt hot/cold flashes across her skin and a bubble rising in her throat, so intense that she pressed her hands against her cheeks to keep from squealing. Her reflection in the fish-eye mirror made her head look like a balloon. With mixed elation and trepidation, she opened the message.

Wttym do u get off wrk?

She couldn't help the grin that spread wide.
No way!
Val made a very clear distinction in her mind between real fantasy and make-believe fantasy. A real fantasy was having a secret admirer send her roses. It had never happened, but it seemed within the realm of actual possibility. A make-believe fantasy was winning the lottery. It was statistically possible, but so unimaginably unlikely that she dared not even to

dream of it. Adam Erb asking her for a date definitely belonged in the make-believe category. Incredulous, but still enthusiastic, she typed her response and counted ten seconds before pressing send.

Whodis?

The reply came a split second later.

Moi, Adam ERB, ofc.

Val looked around, suspicious that one of her co-workers might be pranking her. They wouldn't do something so hurtful, would they? She didn't think so, mostly because she doubted that any of them possessed sufficient social media skills to pull it off. Still, Val possessed hard-earned romantic defense mechanisms, and she was not going to fall for a trick.

How do I knw ur rly u?

The response came swiftly.

DUR? This morn, I saw u at D&D drv-thru, I sed u hav a lovely name.

Indeed, that's exactly what Adam Erb had said. When she closed her eyes, she could still hear his words resonating so deep in her ears that she felt echoes meeting in the middle of her head. Throughout the day, Val had looked at the selfie she'd taken with him over and over and over. Each time, after she put her cell phone away, she had to check again to verify the photo was real.

Still, the intensity of her desire was balanced by a cautionary voice that remained unconvinced.

> *PLZTLME wut did I draw on the bag when I handed yur order?*

The answer came so quick, it was almost automatic.

> *;) THNQ.*

Val hugged herself tight to keep her soul from bursting out of her body. She excused herself to a customer at the window and broke into hysterical tears and fits of laughter. Whether it was better to shout the good news for all to hear, or to keep it a secret for herself, she couldn't decide.

Chavonne lifted the microphone on her headset and called to her. "Hey, girl, why yo' actin' so loopy?"

Val wasn't listening and didn't care, anyway. While agitating about how to reply, she received another message.

> *Are u convinced?*
> *Yes!*
> *Can we meet?*
> *Yes!*
> *When?*
> *I dnt knw. Soon. We got pay-it-4wd streak goin. We nrly got the wrld record!*

A minute passed, which, as Val reckoned time, exceeded the lifespan of most memes. In her world, there was no question that couldn't be answered in sixty seconds or less. She shook the phone, as if something might be clogging it. Finally, she broke down and typed.

> *Still there?*
> *So... why dnt u break the streak & ur free 2 meet me?*
> *Srsly?*
> *4 sur. Can u plz do something? I want 2 meet u, but can't w8 til l8tr.*

Val tapped her fingers on the counter, thinking. She'd always imagined that love required sacrifice. She was willing—lord, was she ever willing—but what he'd asked didn't really even feel like hers to give.

Love also requires compromise, right?

She typed.

> *R u sur?*
> *Yes, plz*
> *How?*
> *Just do it*

Val chewed on her lip.

So, this is how it has to be.

He'd asked her to do a lot—assuming she could even pull it off—but, for crying out loud, this was *Adam Erb*.

Why am I wasting time even thinking about it?

She typed.

> *Will do wut I can asap.*

Adam Erb responding by emailing her.

> *<3*

Val gasped. It was almost too much to conceive— Adam Erb had hearted her. She wanted to forward his heart to everybody she knew, via every media voice and vehicle at her disposal. This news qualified as huge, humongous, positively ginormous. It would put her name right at the heart of the next major internet trend in Columbus.

This is what it feels like to be famous.

Her thoughts changed gears immediately, though, as what he wanted her to do would be *really* difficult.

Oh well. Such is the price of fame. Celebrity comes with considerable responsibility.

She accepted the task that Adam had given her as a mission, a quest, a rite of passage, a true test of her courage, her loyalty, and her worthiness. But how could she possibly even do what he asked? The pay-it-forward streak had grown into a beautiful thing, with a life of its own. She visualized it like a friendly dragon with bright eyes, puffy cheeks, and a long, serpentine body that grew and grew from the end. Given that she'd invested so much social capital in getting it started, she would be sad for it to end, especially when they were getting so close to the record. And it would weigh on her conscience, if she had any hand in ending it.

Upon second thought, though, she saw a solution so obvious that she wondered why Adam hadn't come up with it first. When he'd asked her to "do something" to end the streak, perhaps he hadn't quite thought things through. As much as she wanted to stay with her team and stick with the streak until the triumphant finale, she was free to leave at any time. Already, she was working what amounted to unpaid overtime. Sooner or later, the streak would end, anyway.

But Adam Erb may never come calling again.

So, if that's what it takes for me to be with Adam Erb, then I'm ready and willing to walk away from the job, my friends, and the streak. That should be good enough to prove the depth of my devotion, right?

Confident in her decision, she sent him a message.

I am ready 4 u. Can u pick me up?

An immediate response came.

Did u stop the pay-it-4ward? Is it over?
No need. I am leaving b'cuz I choose u. (-:

Val hoped for something dramatically affirmative, like a huge YES in all caps, with hundreds of trailing exclamation marks and maybe an attached animated video with dancing animals and hearts raining down from the sky.

Seconds passed. A minute passed.

Val told herself to be patient—*maybe he's searching for just the right words*—but the waiting began to feel all too familiar. She knew what if felt like to be stood up. Finally, the message arrived.

WTF! U gotta kill the pay-it-4ward, 1st, if u want 2 B with me.

"What the fuck?" Val mouthed silently. Though she possessed a vast capacity for wishful thinking, she wasn't dumb. Clearly, Adam Erb wasn't just testing her. He was using her.

Her eyes bulged with pent-up tears, which she held back, save for a single drop sliding down each cheek.

"Wha's s'matter, girl?" Chavonne asked. "Yo' look like somebody done stole yo' lunch money."

"I'm fine," Val said, wiping her cheeks. "I'm just getting tired."

Ximena said, "Then drink up some coffee, *señorita*. We are not finished yet, not by a long shot."

Val pivoted to look away from Chavonne and Ximena, now understanding clearly what she had to do. If Adam required her to sabotage the streak, then that was not too high a price to pay. She would allow herself to be exploited, if that's what it took for her to find happiness.

But how?

The line for the drive-thru stretched so far, she couldn't see the end, and she knew that every single person in it awaited their turn so that they could participate in the pay-it-forward Christmas miracle. It wasn't like she could just tell them all to go home.

While working at the pickup window, she controlled only a couple parts of the process: handing the orders to customers, and taking their payments. She enjoyed the job—chatting with people, mingling and making small talk, sharing a few laughs and stories, even flirting, just a little. She took pride in believing that her good humor enhanced people's enjoyment, and maybe had even contributed to keeping the streak alive.

Conversely, she wondered how her customers would react if she acted surly or snapped at them. Would being grumpy ruin their experience? Could she offend somebody so much that they'd leave without paying-it-forward? She didn't know if she had it in her to be genuinely rude, but it was the only thing she could think to try.

The next car pulled into the drive-thru, and the driver, a gray-haired woman with yellowish eyes, reminded Val of her mother. Accompanying her in the car were three other women of approximately the same age. One of them had a Bible on her lap.

Val gulped.

Maybe I can try being rude to the next car.

But, no, if she was going to do this, she needed to stifle all pleasant inclinations, harden her heart, and become an actual asshole.

But what makes assholes, assholes? What's their motivation?

Once, she had lost her temper and cursed at her mother. She tried to recall the circumstances....

"Bless you, my dear," the gray-haired woman said to Val when she slid open the window.

Of course!

Her mother had told her that if she wasn't careful, she'd end up an old maid! She remembered that it had made her so angry that she'd said....

"So what's it to you, *bitch*?"

The gray-haired woman's yellow eyes swelled. "Excuse me?"

And then, just as when she'd said those words to her mother, Val broke down and blubbered. "I'm sorry. I didn't mean it. I was just so...."

"So what, my dear?"

"Frustrated!"

The gray-haired woman looked at her companions and said to them, "Well, we all know what that feels like, don't we sisters?"

"Amen!" they all said.

In the end, not only did the gray-haired woman pay-forward for the next person, but gave Val an extra $10 tip and wished her luck "with your problem."

"Damn, girl. Ain't fair that yo' can be so snotty, an' still get good tips," Chavonne complained.

"Maybe you need a break?" Ximena asked her.

"No, no, no, I'm fine," Val replied. Actually, she felt like running straight home, diving into her bed, and pulling the blankets over her head, but she reminded herself that she had to be strong, because anything less than absolute resolve would jeopardize her chance to score a date with Adam Erb. She closed her eyes, scrunched her cheeks, and bit her lips, trying to re-focus.

Clearly, she couldn't break the streak by being obnoxious. She just wasn't constitutionally capable of nastiness. It was a flaw.

But, she was capable of deceit. She'd told little white lies before, like when her mother asked her if a pair of yoga pants looked good on her, and she said yes even though they made her butt look like a pumpkin. So, if she couldn't prevent customers from paying-forward, maybe she could lie about whether they did.

That might work!

Val resolved that she would do everything normally with the next customer, but after completing the transaction and the customer had left, she'd secretly pocket the forward payment and then cry out in despair, for everybody to hear, "Oh no! That last person left without paying-it-forward! I guess that it's over. Too bad."

Afterwards, she would email Adam and tell him that she'd fulfilled her part of the bargain, and now she was ready to come and meet him in a dream.

She leaned out the window to size up the next car as it approached. The PT Cruiser, bright red, had a mini-Mexican flag hanging from the rear view mirror. Beneath the street lights, the kiosk cast a shadow over the driver, so that all Val could see of him was his left arm resting against the driver's side window.

She psyched herself by thinking of Adam Erb, waiting for her in his limo, with a bouquet of red roses and a bottle of champagne.

Thank God I'm wearing Skivvies!

You can do this, she told herself. She practiced sleight of hand by palming a sugar packet, as if it was cash put down on the counter to pay-it-forward. She surprised herself at how quickly she could pocket the contraband, but she'd never stolen anything in her life. So, rather than steal outright, she promised herself that when nobody was looking, she'd slip that money into the tips jar. That way, just as everybody shared the tips, so would everybody share some small part in ending the streak, too.

Once she'd made up her mind, she forced any second thoughts straight out of her head.

The car stopped inches from the pickup window. Although she was looking over the top of the vehicle to avoid its driver's eye, she was nevertheless listening intently.

"*Buenas noches,* my friend."

The man's voice, gentle yet melodic, spoke with a flair for poetry. It conveyed a warmth that embraced Val, like a soft kiss against her earlobes, delicate fingers running through her hair. To hear it felt like awakening from a pleasant dream. It was familiar, comforting, alluring, but Val couldn't quite place it.

"Tonight is a miracle, do you not agree?"

Then it hit , literally, like a wakeup call. It was the same voice in the clip that she'd uploaded for her morning alarm, the same dulcet yet masculine inflection that eased her into each new day. She'd know it anywhere.

"Huh?" was all that Val could manage.

From inside the store, Ximena cried, "Mateo! You have come!"

Her exclamation was followed by squeals and giggles from the children. They all hastened to the pickup window, Ximena and Tatiana squeezing on one side of Val, Ignacio and Babette on the other.

"Do you, uh, know this customer?" Val asked.

"*Si*, he is my *hermano*, Mateo. I asked him to come here." Ximena squirmed her arms and torso through the window to hug him. "I was worried you would not come, because of this weather."

Mateo leaned forward into the light. He had a pencil-thin mustache.

Val was sure that she'd seen him in a movie, somewhere.

"I came because you asked, darling sister. This storm is not so bad."

The way he enunciated "darling," as if it were a word from a prayer, made Val's legs shake.

"Eh, then. After you have paid-forward your part, go park your car. Come in and visit with us for a time."

"I will," Mateo said to Ximena. He then reached forward, grazing Val's sleeve. "Would you be so kind to hand me my order?"

Too stunned to speak, Val didn't respond verbally, although she smiled when she creased the top of the bag and gave it to Mateo. He said *gracias* and handed her a $20 bill so crisp, Val imagined hers and his were the only two hands ever to have held it.

"Please use the change to pay forward something nice for the next person." He winked, then slowly rolled up the window and drove off.

Ximena snapped her fingers in front of Val's face. "Wake up, girl. You should really take a break."

"Yeah, I think you're right." Val rubbed the currency between her thumb and index finger, and asked Ximena, "By any chance, has your brother ever done any professional voice work?"

"Oh, he does have a beautiful voice. I don't know. It is possible. Why do you not ask him? I will introduce you."

"I couldn't ask... that is, I don't want to... uh, impose," Val stammered. "You're right. I think I do need a break."

She backed away from the window, feeling as if slowly coming out of a trance. She pushed her way through milling bodies, losing her bearings a couple of times before she found the door to the restroom and staggered in. Once inside, she gazed at the wall of urinals and said, "Oh shit."

Her heart pounding, she collapsed inside a stall and sat with her back to the tank, legs straddling the sides of a toilet. She rolled a huge wad of toilet paper into her hand, just waiting for the tears to burst out of her eyes. Instead, not even one drop of leakage came. It felt as though she'd already cried herself out. For several seconds, she stared at the back of the stall door, where somebody had scrawled in marking pen: *Roxy gives good head.*

She didn't know who Roxy was, but, figuring that she wouldn't want such things written about her in a men's room, she wetted the toilet paper and began rubbing out the graffiti.

When she finished, she took her cell phone, opened the last text from Adam Erb, and replied to his message.

I couldn't do it. I'm sorry.

Adam replied immediately.

Too bad 4 u.

Val flushed the toilet just to hear it, because the sound of it captured her feelings at that moment.As the water swirled, she copied her entire thread of correspondence with Adam Erb, from *Wttym do u get off wrk?* to *Too bad 4 u,* and she posted everything to every social media venue at her disposal.

CHAPTER 18

6:30 PM

Jay-Rome had felt somewhere between relieved, confused, and dissed when Adam Erb left the Polaris Drip 'n' Donuts with Jack Gentile in Jack's limo.

He'd strolled right by Jay-Rome, waving him away and dismissing him summarily by saying, "Go home and keep my old man company."

"Say huh, boss?"

"Just do whatever makes the geezer happy," Adam had said as he climbed into Jack's vehicle.

As they drove away, Clarence Bone honked and thumbed his nose at Jay-Rome.

The crass send-off felt a little like getting dumped. It especially stung after they'd seen and done so many unusual things on that day. Jay-Rome took pride in believing that he'd not only driven Adam from one destination to the next, but that, through his wit and insight, he'd contributed to their adventures. Deep down, every driver harbored a belief that his client needed him for more than just transportation, and that, perhaps at some unconscious level even deeper down, the client knew it. So long as he believed that they shared that unspoken code of understanding, Jay-Rome could tolerate how Adam occasionally treated him like a peasant. Suddenly abandoning him in the cold like that was just plain hardhearted, though. It violated the code.

Jay-Rome felt like he'd earned the right to see where that day's odd travels finally ended.

He'd always known that Adam was an asshole — actually one of his more endearing qualities. It imposed limits on his vanity. While Adam undeniably had a golden touch when it came to making money, he couldn't make himself any less of an asshole. He thus needed Jay-Rome to indirectly, through irony and inquiry, remind him of that fact, lest he begin to believe his own bullshit. For example, once, when Adam was late for an appointment, Jay-Rome helpfully reminded him that, on one hand, the meeting couldn't begin until he arrived, but on the other hand, nobody really wanted him there, anyway. That was the kind of value-added service any good driver provided.

Jay-Rome felt that it was not only rude, but also a serious mistake for his boss to banish him at such a critical moment in that day. Adam may not have realized it, but he was tiptoeing through a quagmire of his own bullshit, and he needed Jay-Rome to help him navigate through it without falling face-down into the filth. That knowledge accounted for the part of Jay-Rome that felt relieved. All in all, that part might have been just a hair greater than the parts that felt jilted or confused.

Besides, playing poker with Ernest proved a more pleasant way to spend a stormy evening. Since Ernest couldn't lift or hold the cards, they'd worked out a system. Jay-Rome dealt the cards facing Ernest, putting them upright in a Scrabble letter tray in front of him. It sometimes took the old man a few minutes to assess his draw, but when he did, he'd grunt to indicate how many replacement cards he wanted. Jay-Rome dealt them in the same fashion as before, then pointed to each card in the tray until Ernest indicated which ones to discard.

After a couple of minutes, Jay-Rome started the bidding. "I'm putting down two chips," he said.

Ernest grunted three times.

"So, then, you match me and raise one chip. I'm cool with that, but I'm gonna let my nuts hang a little lower. I match and raise you two more chips."

Ernest rolled his tongue and emitted a raspberry.

"Okay, so you call." Jay-Rome fanned his cards on the table. "I got two pairs, deuces and jacks."

"Hraaaahraaaah," Ernest hooted, his way of laughing.

Jay-Rome turned Ernest's card tray around – it contained three of a kind, aces.

"Damn your old stinkin' ass," Jay-Rome cursed, pushing the chips toward Ernest. "I can't ne'er tell if you are bluffing, or if you are just ugly."

"Hraaaahaaaah."

Jay-Rome never actually *let* the old man win, but neither did he try too hard to beat him. He couldn't help feeling sorry for him. All day long, every day, so long as Ernest was awake and, often, even while he was napping, he sat parked in front of the television in what his son euphemistically called the "sun" room, but which everybody knew was really his sick room. Jay-Rome suspected that it drove him the old man nuts – news, the morning talk shows, game shows, reruns, soap operas, more talk shows, more news, all leading up to prime time features that were all some manner of contrived competition between survivors, suitors, or singers. This functioned as both a sensory assault and a mental insult, but when Ernest tried to complain that it was all bull-fucking-shit, it came out sounding, "brrrl fah fah fah ooog uhk ooog uhk ng ng ng sneeeet." Only Jay-Rome understood this new language.

Still, Ernest pitched a fit if anybody ever turned off the TV. It was embedded in his reality, an anchor for his rambling mind.

While they played, Jay-Rome turned down the volume to a whisper, but even at a mere murmur, Ernest seemed to always be listening, ready to call out bull-fucking-shit if he heard something he didn't like.

So, when a special breaking news report interrupted the regular programming, he called to Jay-Rome, "Uh pah!"

"You want me to turn the sound up?"

When Jay-Rome pointed the remote at the TV, he, too, started paying attention. "Whoa. That there is my girl."

And so it was, reporting live: "This is D'Nisha Glint on the north side of the city, in the parking lot outside of the Drip 'n' Donuts store on Cleveland Avenue. There have been new developments in a story from earlier today, about a pay-it-forward line of customers that has been going continuously since 6:00 AM. At Eyewitness News, we've learned that the streak is now approaching a world record. I'm speaking to you from inside our mobile news van because, as you can see...."

The camera panned the expanse of the parking lot, where a caravan of cars queued, then up and down Cleveland Avenue, pausing to show the traffic lights swaying in the driving wind and snow, before turning back to the storefront and the crowds assembled inside and outside.

"...there is such a massive crowd and traffic jam that it's difficult for us to get our van any closer. The wind chill is currently negative twenty degrees outside, and yet, still, people are coming, despite the weather, despite up-to-an-hour wait, just to get donuts. The store manager, Mr. Huck Carp, told me via Skype that within the hour, he projects that they will have broken the world record. And there is no end in sight."

"Sizzling titties!" Jay-Rome exclaimed. "Ain't that something jeezy? Who woulda done thought that business would still be goin' down?"

Ernest lifted his left arm with his right arm and pointed with his pinky finger. "Annaaaa waaaana gug."

"Say huh? You wanna go there?"

"Ya."

"Naw. We can't leave. It's cold 'nuff to freeze Rudolf's red asshole out there. Boss would drop a cow if I took you out on a night like this."

On the television, D'Nisha Glint continued. "I'm here with Bartleby Fusco, who is the security guard at the strip mall. Tell me, Mr. Fusco, have you ever seen anything like this?"

"No way! If I didn't know better, I'd think it was the second coming of our Lord and Savior, Jesus Christ, right here in Columbus. My momma always said that if Jesus ever came to Columbus, he'd like it here."

"Yes. Right. But I suppose that there have been some challenges, what with so many people assembled in one place."

"Not so much as you'd think. People are behaving themselves. It's like folks are trying to prove themselves worthy of all this charity."

"Yes. Right. But I do see that there is a police presence across the street."

The camera zoomed across Cleveland Avenue, where two state highway patrol cars idled next to a long black limousine, like dignitaries in a private booth watching a parade.

Flubber looked as if he hadn't notice them prior to that moment. "I guess they're keeping an eye, just in case."

Upon seeing the police cruisers, Ernest started trembling, then shaking, then rocking in his chair as if shot full of adrenaline. He puffed his chest so wide that the badge pinned to his robe popped off.

"We are thankful for their presence," D'Nisha added.

Leaning forward, stretching, twisting, and reaching, Ernest put his hand on the television flat screen, and he squawked, "Annaaaa waaaana gug gug gug."

"Oh," Jay-Rome said, tapping a finger to his forehead. "You wanna go there?"

"Ya ya ya ya ya...."

"That ain't a great idea."

"Grrrrrr...."

"Well, Boss Man did give me 'pecific instructions that I should make you happy. I guess this would qualify." He grabbed hold of the handles of Ernest's wheelchair. "Let's get on your hat and coat, and we'll bust ass getting to Cleveland Avenue."

Ernest spontaneously cheered a loud and perfectly articulate, "Boo yah!"

CHAPTER 19

6:55 PM

"Why can't you just arrest them?"

"It's like I explained, sir...."

Adam Erb stretched across Jack's whole body to look the state highway patrol officer in the eye, even though she wore impenetrable dark glasses.

Two officers stood outside of the limo, looking down at him through the cracked window on Jack's side of the limo. Despite the icy wind and knifing snow, they stood stoically, one woman and one man, in their dark gray shirts and trousers, razor brimmed hats, shiny utility belts, and black blazers with a winged tire logo on the shoulder patches — no coats, not even bullet-proofed vests, which Adam rather thought that the situation warranted, as a precaution. Their faces didn't flinch. Adam wondered if they were even able to feel the cold.

The taller of the two — the woman — did all the talking. "...The crowd is orderly. Traffic is congested but moving. We have no reason to suspect that any crime is being committed."

"What about my stolen delivery truck, huh?"

"Actually, Adam, that was *my* stolen delivery truck," Jack corrected him. "And that might have been a misunderstanding, which I will settle later. But for now, I do not intend to press any charges."

Adam ignored Jack's remarks, elbowed him aside, lowered the window all the way, and stuck his head and shoulders outside. He could have reached out and grabbed the officer's gun, but shook that idea out of his head. "So you are just going to stand by and watch? I can smell the weed form here."

"Possession of small amounts of marijuana has been decriminalized in Ohio. Smoking it in public is illegal, but these circumstances do not rise to the level to warrant police action. For us to break up the proceedings would be far more dangerous than for us to allow them to continue."

"So what do you intend to do, officer?"

"We will monitor the situation," she said, taking one step backwards.

"Let's get some donuts," the other trooper said.

"Leave the matter to us, gentlemen. We suggest that you go home."

Adam opened his mouth to object, until Jack started closing the window, which rose like an upside down guillotine rising under his neck. Adam wrenched his head free and said, "Don't tell me that you agree with them?"

"Whether I agree or disagree is irrelevant," Jack said, "because they are the Ohio State Patrol. What they say, goes."

"Bah. Scumbags."

Adam's cell phone trilled an incoming message. He opened the message manager, noted that he had over 200 recent unread postings in which he'd been tagged, then closed the app and mumbled, "For crying out loud."

A flurry of wind blew under the car and made a whistling noise as it sifted through exhaust pipes and shock absorbers. Jack pressed his ear to the window, listening.

"Do you hear that?"

"What? The wind?"

"It sounds like a song."

Jack began humming *Santa Claus is Coming to Town.*

"Really? Are you drunk, Jack?"

"I'm trending in that direction."

"How can you be so cavalier about everything?"

"There's nothing to do, Adam. If you insist on staying, despite what the police officers recommend, then we might as well make ourselves comfortable." Jack loosened his collar and began crooning, "You'd better watch out. You'd better not cry...."

Jack's voice sounded as though he was gargling with sour milk. Listening to him was torture, but Adam refused to show his irritation.

"I just wish I knew what the hell is going on in there," he said.

6:56 PM

Ximena shepherded her brother Mateo around the shop to meet all of her friends and colleagues on the Drip 'n' Donuts staff.

When introduced to Val, he said, "It is a pleasure to meet you."

Val blushed and replied, "*El placer es todo mio, señor.*"

"Since when do you speak Spanish?" Ximena asked, astonished.

"*Hablo español cuando hablo con un caballero,*" she replied, more to Mateo than to her. "But, really, I mostly just speak online Spanish. I have lots of Latino friends. I also speak some online French, German, and Japanese. Google translate helps a lot."

"*Es asombroso!*" Ximena declared. "Maybe I should not say so often to Tatiana that the computer wastes her time."

"*Serias mi amigo de Facebook, señorita?*" Mateo asked.

"*Si por supuesto,*" Val replied. "I'll send you a friend request."

Finally, when Mateo left, he took Ignacio and Babette with him, promising Ximena that he'd put them to bed, since she was not able to predict when she'd be home.

Earlier, Tatiana had asked Ximena for permission to stay until... well, at least until they broke the world record. At the time, Ximena had said, "We shall see," even though in her mind she was elated that her daughter had proposed anything approximating a shared activity. As soon as Mateo was out the door, Ximena turned to Tatiana and said, "If you are going to stay with us, you must work."

"Work? Will I be paid?"

"Haven't you already eaten a day's wages worth of donuts?"

"What would you have me do?"

"Something simple. Maybe you could wash dishes."

At home, doing the dishes was Tatiana's most hated chore. So when she squawked, "No way," Ximema was prepared to counter offer.

"Well, so... what do you think you would be able to do?"

Tatiana looked around to see who seemed to be having the most fun. Ximena had maneuvered their conversation to be near the orders work station, where Chavonne was humming to herself while taking an order from a customer.

"There," Tatiana pointed. "I could wear the headphone and be the person who talks to people when they enter the drive-thru."

"No, I don't think so. To wear the technology, you must be very skilled."

"I can do it!"

"I don't know...."

"Let me prove it to you!"

"Very well. If you think that you are capable of learning very quickly, I give you permission to ask Miss Chavonne if she would mind letting you work at her job for a while."

"Hell no!" Chavonne answered without waiting to be formally asked. "I'm all about sharing the joy."

Ximena took the headset from Chavonne and placed it delicately on Tatiana's head, as if it was a crown. "Here, *princessa*. Let me show you how this works."

6:57 PM

"What's that?" Chavonne asked. She'd been lurking behind Huck, eavesdropping over his shoulder while he worked on his tablet.

He invited her to sit next to him. "It's a spreadsheet. I use it for keeping track of forward payments."

"A sheet? Sounds like what's something yo'd put on top of a bed. What for do yo' need to make it so complicated?"

Huck frowned. "There are many variables. For example, what if one customer pays forward two fritters and a small black coffee, but the next person wants two glazed donuts and large vanilla chai cooler. What's the difference?"

"Eighteen cents," she answered without hesitation.

"Huh?"

After he'd finished entering the amounts into the corresponding cells on his spreadsheet, he pushed enter and the answer came back: eighteen cents.

"And by adding that into the daily total of what's carried forward in that scarecrow account of yo's, it comes to $428.26."

"You mean the escrow account. But how'd you do that?"

"I done been juggling budgets and floating checks since I was sixteen. Living from paycheck to paycheck, yo' gotta think quick to stretch that money out. I do it all in my head."

"That's impressive."

Chavonne patted herself on the shoulder. "Ain't nobody ever gonna flim flam me. Not even yo' own self."

"Me?"

"Yeah so. I ciphered that after yo' pay off the day shift what they is owed, at their salaries what range from $10.50 to $16.75 per hour, minus Mrs. Johar, who I figure loses her $22 per hour because of her skipping out, as of right this moment yo' got leftover $326.59 in that extra account. And that don't even include tips, which I ain't counted but figure to be somewhere around two hundred bucks. The longer the streak goes, the more free cash there is for all of us to take home."

Huck rubbed his chin. "I was thinking about donating the auxiliary funds to charity, maybe something like the ACLU."

"Don't talk to me 'bout no charity. Ain't yo' ever heard of overhead? Administrative costs? We are owed us something for keeping everything goin' all day long."

"I'm not sure that's ethical."

"Please!" Chavonne took Huck by the hand. "Don't talk no shit like ethics. I'm poor, but I got my own dreams, Huck. They cost some money. I can't earn enough for them workin' at Drip 'n' Donuts. So they won't come true if not for tips, found money, and maybe winning the lottery."

"Fair enough," Huck said, convinced.

"Finally!" Chavonne offered Huck a high five. "Ain't often happen that something happens in this world that is both good and fair at the same time."

6:58 PM

At the pickup window, Val worked one-handed because she held her cell phone in the other hand, unwilling to let go for even a second. She'd started offering to take selfies of customers as they passed through the pay-it-forward as a souvenir, kind of the way they did at Cedar Point for riders of the Millennium Roller Coaster, only she gave the pictures to them for free. All she asked in return was that they "friend" her on Facebook. In the process of taking and sharing so many photos, not to mention posting regular updates of her drive-thru encounters and progress toward the world record, her phone constantly chirped to alert her to incoming messages from fans, friends, followers, well-wishers, and admirers.

This was how Val imagined heaven—sort of—not that she really thought about it all that much, at least not enough to have decided whether she believed in it or not... but if she did, she couldn't imagine anything closer to rapture than this. Here, at this moment and in this place, she was the center of attention within an amicable network of fellow geeks, gamers, techies, twitterati, and their avatars. They responded to everything she posted as if it were Scripture. She'd originated three simultaneously trending hash tags, the busiest of which had emerged in response to material that she'd posted about her text exchange with Adam Erb. The people were on her side, offering support, encouragement, and even dates, which more than helped to mend her broken heart.

Paradise was like riding the crest of a great internet trend; it didn't matter that it might crash and be forgotten in ten minutes time, for in that instant, she surfed atop the leading edge of a hash-tagged tsunami. She could live in the memory of that moment for the rest of her life.

6:59 PM

In between tunes, while members of the Bottom Dwellers' jam session chatted, laughed, played grab-ass, and passed a variety of mind-altering substances, Edgar stepped forward, alone, and started playing a plaintive tune on his old fiddle. From the kitchen, Tank heard it and thought he recognized it. He left the Turbo Chef oven counting down, and went to listen. He closed his eyes, the better to let the music seep into his head.

An aching feeling from his past came out in the form of song, his voice a deep, twangy baritone.

> *I... am a man... of constant sorrow...*
> *I've seen trouble all my day.*

Edgar fiddled to match Tank's languorous pace. Eileen grabbed her banjo, and other musicians joined in, too.

> *For six long years... I've been in trouble...*
> *No pleasures here... on Earth I've found.*

Scooter Opalisnky drifted out of the office and started harmonizing in a squeaky but uninhibited voice.

> *It's fare thee well... my old lover...*
> *I never expect... to see you again.*

Soon, everybody in the shop was playing an instrument, singing along, humming, clapping, or snapping their fingers in synch with Tank's lead. He projected his voice so that people heard it on the patio, where they held lighters, torches, flashlights, or other burning materials to show their appreciation and solidarity.

People in line for the drive-thru started honking their horns, probably not even knowing why.

Tank advanced into the center of the floor, put one foot up on a chair, made a fist with one hand, and opened the other arm at full extension to his side.

> *You can bury me... in some deep valley...*
> *For many years... where I may lay.*
> *Then you may learn... to love another...*
> *While I'm sleeping... in my grave.*

When he was finished, he dropped his head and held it down for several seconds.

Nobody breathed.

Finally, the Turbo Chef oven counted down to zero and started beeping. Tank belched, and everybody else gasped.

"Excuse me," he said, wiping his mouth. "Me and that song go back a long way."

7:00 PM

"Shiznet," Jay-Rome muttered to himself. "I can't even see no end to this line."

He approached from Innis Road, and had to strain his neck and turn his head to see the entirety of the expanding pay-it-forward motorcade. Its main channel at the entrance to the mall split onto both the north- and south-bound lanes on Cleveland Avenue, including several meandering tributaries across the parking lot and through alleys and side streets, all converging as if into a funnel at the entrance to the drive-thru. People advanced by taking turns, first-come first-served, in a self-regulated but glacially slow-moving consecution.

Jay-Rome, however, had anticipated this problem. That's why he'd chosen to drive the fully equipped handicapped accessible van instead of the limousine. Even if he had a thousand dollar bill, he doubted if he could bribe his way to the front of the line a second time. A white van with a wheelchair lift on the side, a stick figure in a circle symbol depicting a person in a wheelchair on the back door, and a blue and red emergency flasher on the dashboard, however, might encourage some sympathetic good Samaritan to let him jump the line.

Ernest Erb, strapped around the legs, hips, and chest, with his head propped up by layers of pillows, seemed to be enjoying the adventure. He babbled rhythmically, as if a happy tune was rippling through his head—maybe a Christmas carol.

Jay-Rome thought it kind of sounded like *The Little Drummer Boy*.

"Bah urg ba bum bum, urg ba bum bum, urg ba bum bum...."

Jay-Rome weaved and dodged through rows of cars and the spaces between them to get as close to the front of the queue as possible, and he parked there, waiting, looking for a kind soul to grant him a favor. He put on a sad face and motioned palms-up to other drivers, hoping for somebody's charity. He inched closer, trying to nudge a corner of his van's bumper between two vehicles in the line.

They honked at Jay-Rome, scolded him with wagged fingers, and pointed backwards, to the rear of the line. Some drivers pressed their hands together and bowed their heads as if to say, "sorry," but after having waited sometimes for over an hour to reach that point, they seemed disinclined to give up their places in line for anything short of a medical emergency. The more Jay-Rome tried to squeeze in, the closer the successive cars stuck to one another, front to back, leaving not even a crack into which he could advance.

He was beginning to think that he'd have to backtrack and start over, when he noticed a state highway patrol cruiser moving forward in the line, a dozen or so cars away.

"They say 'protect and serve,' ain't that right?" he said to Ernest. "Let's see if I can convince them that we're worth some of that service." He flipped the switch on the van's emergency flashers to attract their attention.

A female trooper exited the cruiser and approached the van, aiming a high-beam flashlight straight at him.

He pressed his fists into his eyes to make them look red, and let his cheeks sag. "Look miserable," he said to Ernest before rolling down the window.

"Is there some problem, sir?" the trooper asked, looking into the vehicle.

"Yes, ma'am, there is something wrong, and I do hope that you can help us. My patient here, he's really very sick and needs to get home, so we can fix him up with an IV and put him to bed...."

Ernest moaned a shrill lamentation that sounded like a dying coyote with its leg in a trap.

"...But when he learned about this magical pay-it-forward thing what's happening here tonight, he said that he just had to come. I tried to tell him, no, you're not up to it, but he said that this is once in a lifetime, and if it should happen that this is his last Christmas here on Earth, he wants to make it count for something special. So what could I do? Deny him? No, I bundled him up and brought him.

"Still, I'm dreadful worried that he's too weak to wait in this line for such a long, long time. Do you think, officer, under the circumstances, in the spirit of the season, you could see fit to let us budge the line? My patient really wants to do his part to keep the streak going. But it shouldn't be necessary for him to risk catching his death of a cold, don't you think?"

The trooper lifted her clip-on sunglasses, displaying bright blue eyes that twinkled, like an elf's. She looked Ernest up and down, sizing up the extent of his disabilities. "Are you well, sir?

Ernest sighed piteously.

"Did I also mention, officer," Jay-Rome jumped in, "that my patient is a retired police officer, with over 30 years on the force?"

The trooper gazed at the long line of cars behind her, as if weighing the good done to one person against the collective inconvenience of everybody else, then said, "Very well. I'll let you in line ahead of my vehicle."

With gloved hand, she saluted Ernest Erb. "Merry Christmas to you, sir."

7:01 PM

"Go on, Mr. Gentile," Clarence Bone egged him on. "Tell me more."

Jack started pouring another VSOP. When Adam tried to prevent him by covering the glass with his hand, Jack just kept pouring on top of his knuckles. Enough cognac leaked through for a shot, which Jack quaffed.

"Don't you think you've had enough, Jack?"

"Don't be such a pussy."

"You're embarrassing yourself. You're embarrassing me. Your driver doesn't need to hear those stories."

Jack slapped Adam on the leg and asked, "Do you remember the time you let Brenda Bushmeyer give you a vodka enema in the back room of the Sugar Shack?"

Clarence Bone puckered his lips and made the sound of a siphon.

"Shut up, Jack."

"We were a couple of dumbasses back then, but mostly you. I wish I had pictures. I'd put them on Instagram."

"Maybe we should just give up and go home."

"I don't think, not so yet. I'm kinda having fun, yeah. Aint you? You just need to loosen up. Do some more drinking."

"No, I—" Adam's cell phone chirped another incoming message. "Not now," he groused.

"Your phone wants to say something to you, buddy. You've been getting lots and lots of notices. Why aren't you checking them? It ain't like you not to twitter a tweet unanswered."

Adam held his cell phone in the fingertips of his left hand, like something delicate. He glanced at the status line at the top of the screen.

"Holy shit. I've got two hundred and fifty two unread postings. That's way more than normal."

He poised his finger above the screen, but held back opening the news feed; he didn't have the energy or the proper attitude for responding to whatever trivialities his minions were so eager to share with him.

"Fuck 'em," he said.

Jack snatched the phone from Adam's hands and playfully held it beyond his reach, as if playing keep-away. Adam lunged for it but missed and wound up straddling Jack's lap. In dodging him, Jack inadvertently swiped the screen with his thumb, releasing the pent-up deluge of tweets. He started reading.

"Son of a fuck yo' momma upside down, Adam! You gotta read some of the shit people are saying about you. There's a hashtag naming you, #ERB=SCROOGE."

"What? Let me see!"

"Don't let them trolls get to you. Hey, what's this? Here's another hashtag, #ERB=GRINCH."

"Give me my phone back!"

"And another, #ERB=KRAMPUS. Wow, Adam, you are like, man, getting torched on social media. It's because of that girl at Drip 'n' Donuts, the one you tried to bribe. She posted all of your texts everywhere. The comments are, uh, kind of severe."

Jack tossed the phone to Adam as if it were contaminated.

"That bitch!" Adam grimaced so hard that his cheek bones jutted out and his brow twisted into knots. "That backstabbing whore!"

As he read more, his nostrils began to throb and sinuous veins protruded on each temple.

"I'll fix her ass. I'll deny everything. I'll say that she's a stalker. My followers will believe me."

"Do you want a drink now?"

"Fuck yes!"

Jack poured three fingers and handed the glass to Adam, who returned it to him, saying, "Fill it to the brim. I need to bring out my evil side."

"That's the Adam Erb I know, full of Christmas venom."

From past experience and various infamies that he tried to forget, Adam knew very well that he could not hold his liquor. A single swallow of potent spirits had the nearly immediate effect of imbuing him with supreme confidence and absolute certainty, no matter what the situation. Those attributes, added to an already formidable ego, compelled him to act with daring impunity. At its best, alcohol nurtured a sense of righteous indignation. Used scrupulously, it enabled him to do unscrupulous things. At its worst... well, it made him prone to acting not only unscrupulously, but like a bonafide asshole. He could never predict in advance whether the catharsis that alcohol induced in him would be worth the subsequent regrets it might cause. That night, though, he didn't care.

Jack sang out, "He's gonna find out who's naughty and nice."

Adam started composing a response for Twitter. He paused and asked Jack, "Should I call that girl a scabby worm-infested cunt? Is that over the top?"

"A bit, perhaps."

"Maybe I'll start by just calling her a cunt."

"Good thinking."

Adam wanted to vilify Val in the most malevolent way possible. What could he tweet about her? She wore Skivvies made of barbed wire! She was the antidote to Viagra! She was a clit, a skank, a tease, and a bitch! None of those statements seemed to go far enough, though. He slapped himself, trying to inspire even greater malice in his soul. When that didn't work, he stepped out of the car and faced the blizzard. The wind-driven grains of snow felt like miniscule shards of glass, and the penetrating cold slashed into his pores and spread across his whole body. It was painful. It felt exhilarating.

"Get back in, you numbnuts," Jack called to him.

Adam didn't go back in. The cold electrified him, the wind in his face so strong that it made it impossible to blink. When he looked around, the blur of headlights and brake lights vanished so far into the distance that their light seemed redshifted. He turned his head away from the illusion, focusing instead on the lights twinkling and throbbing around the Drip 'n' Donuts. There he noticed the state troopers' cruiser in the drive-thru line... and just in front of it in the line, a van that was familiar from its size, shape, and the large, wheelchair accessible symbol on its side.

"What in the fuck is going on here!" he hollered into the canyons of Cleveland Avenue. "That's my old man's van!"

"Are you getting back in, or not?" Jack asked again.

Adam beat his chest and spit ice into the wind.

"Suit yourself," Jack said, closing the door.

Adam started punching the air. Internal flames ignited by rage and booze propelled his animus outward, while the blizzard squalls slapped him backwards. It felt as if he were engaged in hand-to-hand combat with an invisible adversary. In a fit, he broke off an icicle hanging from the rim of a dumpster and began lunging at the space in front of him. The harder he thrust, the dizzier he got. Still, he kept soldiering forward against all resistance, finally reaching the curb at Cleveland Avenue, where he tripped over a large clod of ice and snow left behind by a plough. When he regained his balance, he took out his wrath and frustration by lifting the solid mass above his head and chucking it across the street. It landed with a thud in the middle of a cluster of people gathered around a garbage can fire on the patio of Drip 'n' Donuts.

"Look out!" Adam roared. "I'm coming!"

7:06 PM

Tatiana watched in the fish-eye mirror as the handicapped van rounded the bend and entered the drive-thru. It was almost too big to fit in the narrow lane, and its wheels spun slightly on ice as it advanced. When it stopped crookedly in front of the kiosk, she wondered if it was stuck.

"Welcome to Drip 'n' Donuts," she said into her microphone. "How can I make your evening great?"

There was no immediate answer. Instead, the van pulled forward a bit farther, so that the kiosk speaker aligned with its rear window. An elderly man seated in the back of the van trembled and teetered into view under the dome of the overhead lamps. The old man's head dropped out of the open window and hung limp from a twig-like neck.

Tatiana hoped that he wasn't going to die on her. "May I take your order?"

"Nawwwwrrrring."

Tatiana removed the headset and cried in her little girl voice: "*Mamá.* Help!"

Ximena took over. "Excuse me, sir. I didn't quite get what you said."

"Nawwwwrrrring."

The van's driver opened the door a crack and, cupping his hands around his mouth, yelled against the wind, "He says that he wants nothing."

"Nothing at all."

"Yeah, that's what he's saying."

"Nawwwwrrrring."

Ximena panicked. "Oh, Huck, come here! This customer here says that he wants nothing."

Huck, jamming in the middle of a tune with the Bottom Dwellers, put down his spoons and went to help Ximena.

"This customer says that he wants nothing," she repeated.

Huck shrugged as he took the headset. "I'm sure it's just a misunderstanding," he said hopefully, then lowered its microphone arm in front of his mouth and, in his most cheerful voice, said, "Hello. How can I be of service to you?"

"Nawwwwrrrring."

"You see. We told you," Ximena said.

The enormity of the threat suddenly dawned upon Huck. He loosened his collar, as if it helped him think. "Please pull up to the window," he finally said to the driver.

Discarding the headset, Huck bounded across the floor, elbowed Val out of the way, and positioned himself at the pickup window, watching the van slowly advance. Again, the driver pulled forward far enough so that the van's back seat lined up with the window where Huck was waiting.

The old man's face was contorted in a way that expressed pain, mirth, confusion, mischief, as well as the possibility that he had absolutely no comprehension of where he was or what he was doing. His breath came out in a rancid mist.

"Good evening, sir. Thank you for participating in our pay-it-forward event. The prior customer has already purchased two lemon custard donuts for you...."

"Nawwwwrrrrring!"

"...and, now, the expectation is for you to reciprocate by ordering something for the next customer in line. We're trying to break a world record."

"Nawwww-ring-ring-ring-ring!"

The driver lowered his window and shouted back to Huck, "He says that he don't want nothing, but that's okay. I'll take those donuts and pay something forward for him."

The old man seized. His head rattled around as if held onto his neck by one loose bolt. His shoulders shook violently, while his arms flailed like wet rags. Greenish spittle flew from the corners of his mouth. A wave of stench suggested loss of bowel control. Still, through labored breath, he insisted, "Nawwwwrrrring! Nawwwwrrrriiiinnnnggggg!"

At that instant, Adam Erb burrowed through the crowd loitering around the door and ploughed his way into the shop. He reached the counter and stood there, hyperventilating, arms crossed. The Bottom Dwellers stopped playing right in the middle of *Dance All Night with a Bottle in Your Hand.*

Adam bristled when he saw Val, but then he noticed, behind her at the pickup window...

"Dad!" Adam shouted.

"It's Adam Erb!" Val cried.

"Erb?" Several voices asked, declared, exclaimed, or cursed, each in their own way but all at once.

"Erb is a jerk," Edgar proclaimed.

"He's a dick," Eileen said.

In the next second, after realization set in, somebody booed, and a chorus of catcalls quickly amplified.

"Erb is a dick!"

"Erb is Scrooge!"

"Erb is Grinch!"

"Erb is Krampus!"

"Booooo, Adam Erb!"

Recoiling from the abuse, Adam covered his ears and knocked people out of the way as he barreled toward the pickup window.

Huck stood in his way.

"Move, asshole," Adam ordered.

"Do you have any idea what you're doing?" Huck asked.

"Nawwwwwrrrrring!" the old man moaned.

When Adam tried to swat Huck aside, they got into a scrap. Adam slapped at Huck's face, but missed, and instead knocked a tray with two lemon custard donuts onto the floor. Huck dodged the blow, but landed his left foot on a custard donut and skidded across the tile floor, straight into the open pickup window, where he teetered on the ledge for a moment, and then tumbled head-over-heels all the way outside. As he was falling, he grabbed onto Adam's jacket lapel and pulled him through, too. They landed in a snowdrift by the curb, and they continued wrestling with each other, each trying to get on top but neither able to hold onto the advantage.

A state trooper dashed out of the cruiser and called, "Break it up."

"Boss, yo' better get into the car now," Jay-Rome called to Adam. He hustled out and lifted Adam by the armpits to separate him from the melee.

Huck gave up. With nothing left for him to hold onto, he just let go.

Adam didn't resist while Jay-Rome stuffed him into the passenger's seat of the van and slammed the door behind him. Settling into the seat, Adam patted his pocket and realized that he'd lost his cellphone in the scuffle with Huck.

"Wait," he called, "My cell phone...."

"Boss, we gotta go."

"But what'll I do without it?"

Huck picked up Adam Erb's cell phone and smashed it underfoot.

The driver accelerated so hard that the van spun, then swerved, but finally lurched forward, out of the drive-thru and onto Cleveland Avenue, gone and empty-handed. From the open window in the back of the van, the old man's voice trailed into the distance.

"Nawwwwwrrring!

"Nawwwwwrrrring!

"Nawwwwrrrriiiinnnngggg....."

CHAPTER 20

7:25 PM

For all of its ruckus, passion, promise, and pandemonium, the Columbus Christmas Donut Revolution ended abruptly, then fizzled out quickly. Such is the fate of most would-be revolutions, Huck mused: their ardor peaks, and they're over almost as soon.

Nobody spoke for several seconds after Adam Erb's van drove away, ending the streak. The only commentary was non-verbal: Val sniffled, Ximena sighed, Tank snorted.

Huck suspected they were deferring to him, should he care to issue any final remarks that might lend solace to them or give meaning to the day.

In his guts, Huck felt his emotions bottom out. In his head, his thoughts twisted into knots. In his bones, his resolve shattered into bits. And in his heart, his hopes burst like an over-inflated bubble. Regret stoked a fever of angst and despair that made him sweat from his brow. He blamed Adam Erb, but still, he felt at fault himself — for letting the streak slip away, but also for having allowed himself to believe in miracles.

Upon learning that there was no forward-payment waiting for him, the next customer in the drive-thru also declined to pay-forward. Word that the streak was over — failed, short of the record — spread rapidly, and cars in line began peeling away, no longer interested in participating in anything that wasn't historic. The

Eyewitness News team, which had been prepared to preempt regular programming as soon as the record fell, packed up its equipment and left without so much as a wave goodbye. With nothing left to unite them in purpose or passion, the pilgrims gathered on the patio put out their fires and left for warmer places. The Bottom Dwellers played *The Parting Hand*, then packed up their instruments and left for their next gig, wherever and whenever that might happen.

Within fifteen minutes, the strip mall parking lot sat desolate. Snow had already begun to pile up in the vacant spaces left behind. The lights inside the Drip 'n' Donuts shop crackled, as if stressed by the weight and frigidity of the night.

Scooter Opalinsky came out of, went back into, and came out of the office, all without apparent design. Finally, he rapped his knuckles on the countertop and raised his voice.

"Listen up, people," he said. "You did good a good thing today, but it has been a long day. You're way beyond overtime, and you should all go home. I've called the night shift to come in early. There won't be much business, not on a night like this. Go, now."

Val, Ximena, and Chavonne looked at each other, as if trying to elect a speaker amongst them. Finally, Tatiana, who clung to her mother's arm, said, "So that's it."

Tank untied the apron he'd worn all day. "I'm outta here. I could go for a couple of cold brews at the Zig Zag Club." He chuckled. "But, nah, I think that tonight I'll just go home and watch *The Apprentice* on television. It's a better way to go than getting drunk and passing out in the back of the truck again. Besides, that Trump dude cracks me up."

Val lifted the corners of her mouth in a subtle smile, the way somebody might when thinking about somebody she loves. "I need to log on to my computer at home and begin reading all the chatter in my social media. I have a lot of new friends that I'm anxious to meet."

Ximena put her arm around her daughter. "Tati and I will go home, too. I am tired. And, for her, it is a school night."

Tatiana pulled her mother's hand across her chest. "Goodnight. I like it here. Maybe I can get a job here, someday."

Chavonne clicked her tongue and said, "Yo' all sound beat-up. I ain't tired, not at all one bit. I'm taking my share of the tips and going to the Electric Company. It's still early, and I feel like I might want to dance."

Though everybody had declared their intentions for the rest of the evening, nobody took a step toward acting on them. Huck felt as if they were waiting for him to speak. His thoughts were clogged and jumbled; he couldn't even come up with any relevant socialist quotation that seemed to fit the situation. The only thing clear to him was something he didn't have the guts to say — that he loved them, each and every one. He hoped that they could read it on his face.

"Spill it, kid. What're you going to do?" Tank finally asked.

"I'm quitting."

Huck wasn't sure if he'd spoken those words aloud or if he'd just thought them, until he judged from the others' dumbfounded expressions that it was the former.

"I'm turning in my two week notice, effective now. There's better things that I should be doing."

"What better things do you have in mind?" Scooter asked.

"I'm going back to school. I don't care what it costs. I don't even care if I have to hold my nose and borrow money from some corrupt, fraudulent, usurious, plutocratic lending institution. Later, I'll bring those bastards in the one percent to their knees, after I graduate. But, for now, I've got my own personal revolution to work on."

"I am glad for you," Ximena said.

"We all are," Val concurred.

"Did you know that the company has a scholarship program?" Scooter asked. "It's called The Gentile Fund. I'll put in a good word for you. That is, if I still have a job. Either way, you should apply for it."

"I say that we all should chip in," Chavonne proposed. "Let's give Huck all of that pay-it-forward money left over in his scarecrow account—for his books and such things. It ain't much, but I think that, in a way, it amounts to a different kind of paying something forward."

Huck couldn't speak, so he gestured for everybody to come forward, and as soon as they were within reach, he engulfed them in a group hug. They lingered.

As they slowly broke out of the huddle, they gathered their belongings, put on their coats, and departed into the blizzard, each to their own choices.

Last to leave, Huck bundled up in his coat, scarf, hat, and gloves, but even fortified against the blizzard, his first frigid breath numbed his lungs. He walked in mincing steps on the slippery sidewalk to the bus stop.

He was alone. It occurred to him that there was maybe no lonelier place in all the world than a bus stop on the north side of Columbus, Ohio on a forlorn December night in the middle of a raging tempest. The bus was late. Back to the wind, he felt frost forming on the nape of his neck. Already, his toes were starting to tingle. Then he wondered if the busses were even running on that night, and if not, what would he do.

There's a fear that comes with waiting, the fear that you're alone, that nobody is coming, that nobody cares...

"Need a ride," the old hippie driving a VW van asked as he pulled next to the bus stop.

"Yes, I do."

The old hippie had just visited the Drip 'n' Donuts drive-thru and purchased several large bags of drippies. "Have one," he said.

"Thanks but no thanks."

"Suit yourself. Where are you going?"

"Home. Republic Avenue."

"I'll get you there. But if you don't mind, I've got a couple of quick stops that I need to make along the way."

"Not all all," Huck said, settling in. "There's more than one way to get to where I'm going."

ABOUT THE AUTHOR

Gregg Sapp, a native Ohioan, is a Pushcart Prize-nominated writer, librarian, college teacher and academic administrator. He is the author of the "Holidazed" series of satires, each of which is centered around a different holiday. The first two novels, *Halloween from the Other Side* and *The Christmas Donut Revolution* were published in 2019 by Evolved Publishing. Previous books include *Dollarapalooza* (Switchgrass Books, 2011) and *Fresh News Straight from Heaven* (Evolved Publishing, 2018), based upon the life and folklore of Johnny Appleseed. He has published humor, poetry, and short stories in Defenestration, Waypoints, Semaphore, Kestrel, Zodiac Review, Top Shelf, Marathon Review, and been a frequent contributor to Midwestern Gothic, and others. Gregg lives in Tumwater, WA.

For more, please visit Gregg Sapp online at:
Personal Website: www.SappGregg.net
Publisher Website: www.EvolvedPub.com/GSapp
Goodreads: Gregg Sapp
Twitter: @Sapp_Gregg
Facebook: Gregg.Sapp.1
LinkedIn: Gregg-Sapp-b515921b

WHAT'S NEXT?

Gregg is fast at work on the third book in the "Holidazed" series, and other books will follow that, so please stay tuned to his page at our website to remain up to date:
www.EvolvedPub.com/GSapp

Indeed, the best way to be assured that you won't miss important developments is to subscribe to our newsletter here:
www.EvolvedPub.com/Newsletter

MORE FROM GREGG SAPP

Don't miss Gregg Sapp's award-winning adult tale of an American icon, Johnny Appleseed.

FRESH NEWS STRAIGHT FROM HEAVEN

"I happen to believe that genius makes people weird," a storyteller once said, explaining how Johnny Appleseed could be at once so peculiar and so profound.

Between 1801 and 1812, Ohio and the Old Northwest territory runs wild and brutal, with a fragile peace, savage living conditions, and the laws of civilization far away. Still, settlers stake everything they own on the chance of building better lives for themselves in this new frontier.

John Chapman--aka Johnny Appleseed--knows this land better than any white man. Everywhere he goes, he shares the "Fresh News Straight from Heaven," which he hears right from the voices of angels who chat with him regularly. God had promised him personally that he could build peace by growing fruit.

Convincing people of that vision, though, is no easy task. Most folks consider him mad.

This land teems with a miscellaneous assemblage of soldiers, scoundrels, freebooters, runaway slaves, circuit riders, and religious cultists. Ambitious politicians, like Aaron Burr and William Henry Harrison, dream of creating a new empire there. Meanwhile, a reformed drunkard emerges among the Shawnee as a Prophet, one who spoke with the Great Spirit, Waashaa Monetoo. Along with his brother, the war chief Tecumseh, the Prophet begins building an Indian coalition to take back their land.

Even while the tensions mount, Johnny, with angels urging him on, skates blithely through the crossfire and turmoil, spreading his message, impervious to the mockery and derision being heaped upon him. Finally, however, his faith is challenged when war breaks out in the land, leading to the bloody battle of Tippecanoe between Harrison's army and the Shawnee Prophet's warriors, and ultimately to the declaration of the War of 1812. A violent massacre near the northern Ohio town of Mansfield leaves its citizens terrified and vulnerable.

In a desperate act of faith, Johnny promises the people that he can save them. Thus, he dashes off on a midnight run, seeking to spread peace across a land on the brink of war. With so many lives at stake, Johnny must confront the ultimate test of his convictions.

Hi. Nothing helps an unknown writer more than a reader's rating on Amazon, Goodreads, etc.

Thanks

MORE FROM EVOLVED PUBLISHING

We offer great books across multiple genres, featuring high-quality editing (which we believe is second-to-none) and fantastic covers.

As a hybrid small press, your support as loyal readers is so important to us, and we have strived, with tireless dedication and sheer determination, to deliver on the promise of our motto:
QUALITY IS PRIORITY #1!

Please check out all of our great books, which you can find at this link:
www.EvolvedPub.com/Catalog/

Thank you!